# THE FANTASTICAL WORLD OF BEASTS

STELLA CALDWELL

CARLTON KIDS

# CONTENTS

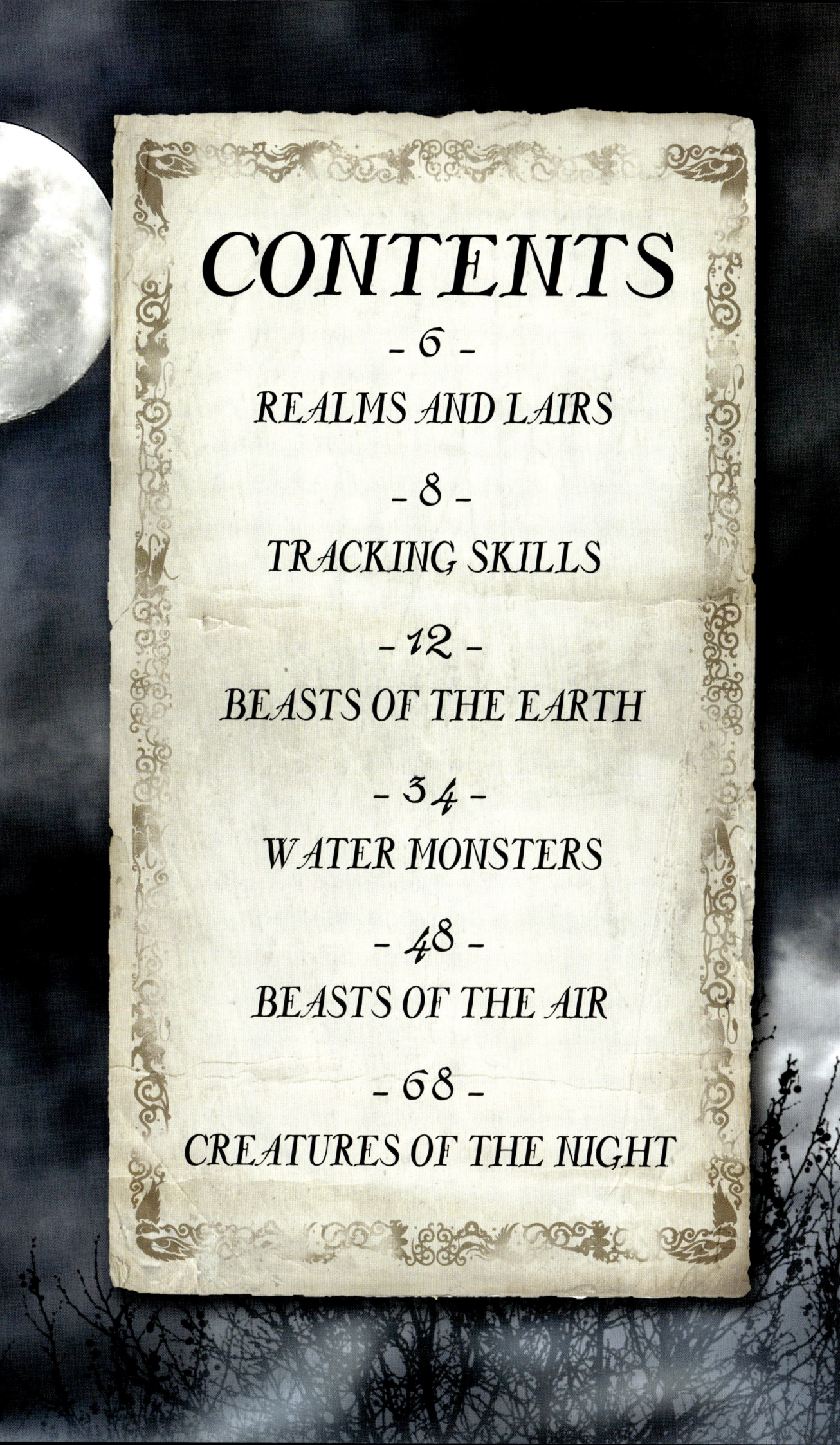

### - 6 -
### REALMS AND LAIRS

### - 8 -
### TRACKING SKILLS

### - 12 -
### BEASTS OF THE EARTH

### - 34 -
### WATER MONSTERS

### - 48 -
### BEASTS OF THE AIR

### - 68 -
### CREATURES OF THE NIGHT

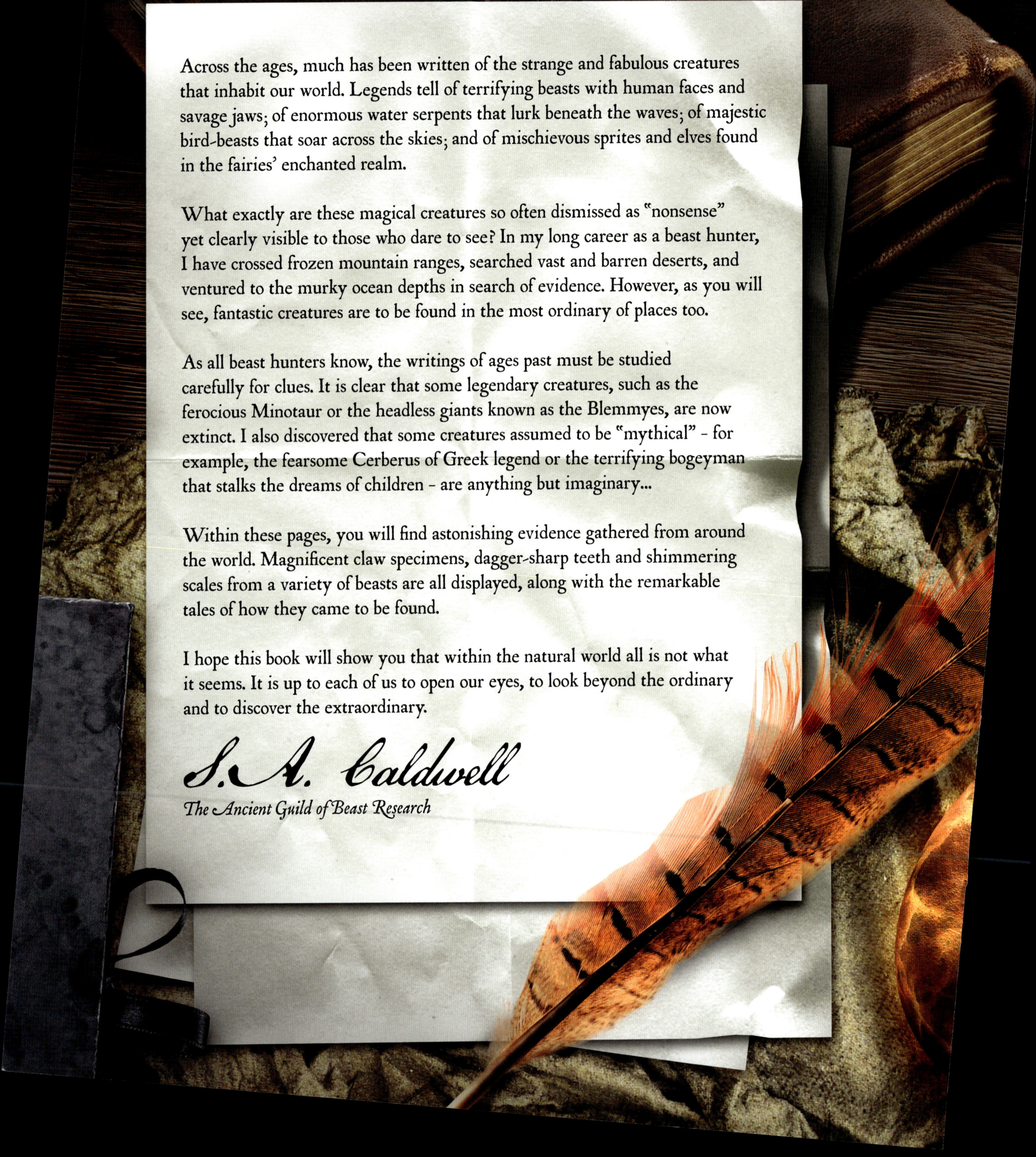

Across the ages, much has been written of the strange and fabulous creatures that inhabit our world. Legends tell of terrifying beasts with human faces and savage jaws; of enormous water serpents that lurk beneath the waves; of majestic bird-beasts that soar across the skies; and of mischievous sprites and elves found in the fairies' enchanted realm.

What exactly are these magical creatures so often dismissed as "nonsense" yet clearly visible to those who dare to see? In my long career as a beast hunter, I have crossed frozen mountain ranges, searched vast and barren deserts, and ventured to the murky ocean depths in search of evidence. However, as you will see, fantastic creatures are to be found in the most ordinary of places too.

As all beast hunters know, the writings of ages past must be studied carefully for clues. It is clear that some legendary creatures, such as the ferocious Minotaur or the headless giants known as the Blemmyes, are now extinct. I also discovered that some creatures assumed to be "mythical" – for example, the fearsome Cerberus of Greek legend or the terrifying bogeyman that stalks the dreams of children – are anything but imaginary...

Within these pages, you will find astonishing evidence gathered from around the world. Magnificent claw specimens, dagger-sharp teeth and shimmering scales from a variety of beasts are all displayed, along with the remarkable tales of how they came to be found.

I hope this book will show you that within the natural world all is not what it seems. It is up to each of us to open our eyes, to look beyond the ordinary and to discover the extraordinary.

*S. A. Caldwell*
The Ancient Guild of Beast Research

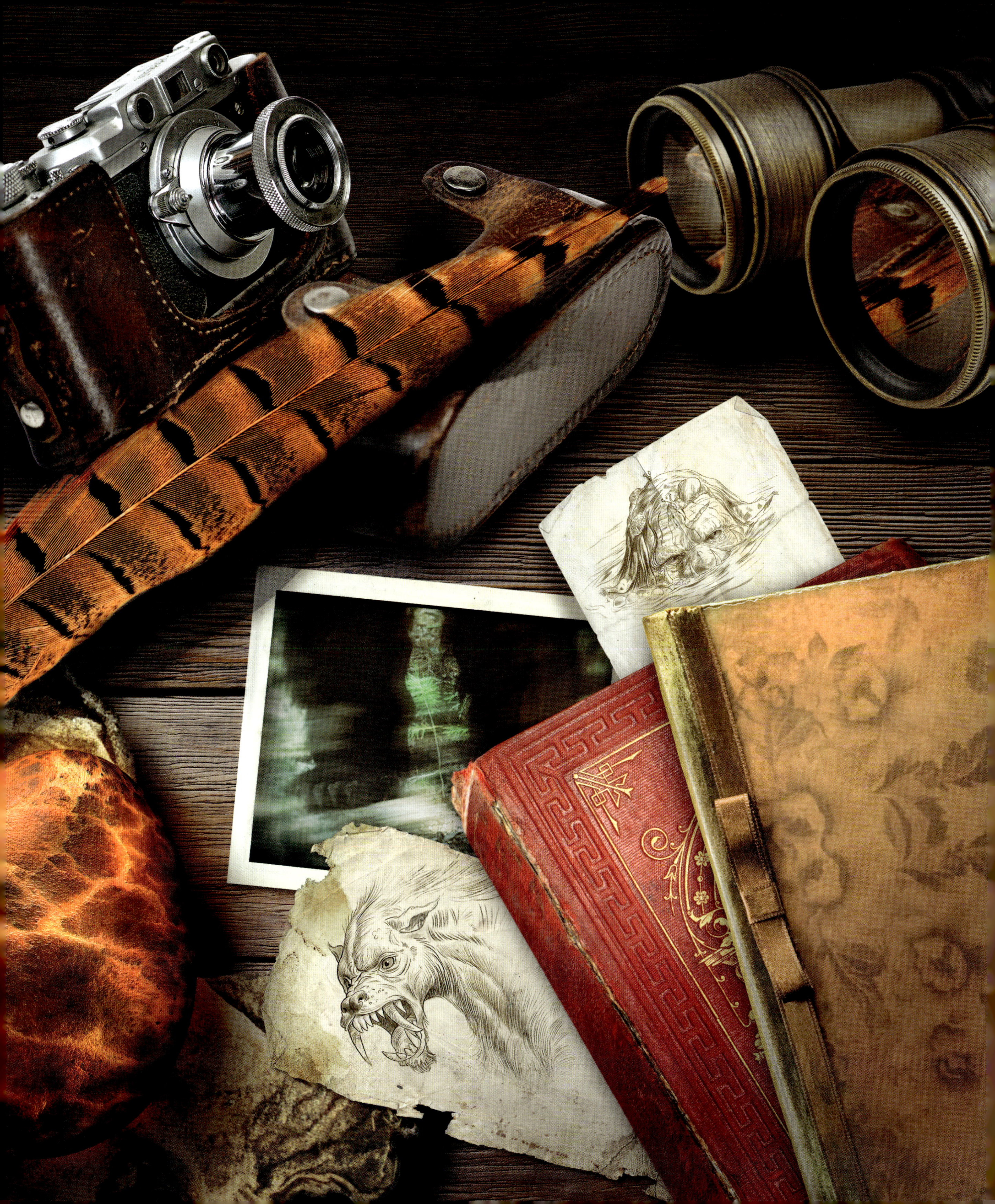

# REALMS and LAIRS

From frozen mountain peaks to murky ocean depths, and from vast deserts to secluded forests, monsters make their homes in an astonishing variety of places. Fantastic beasts may be spotted in the most ordinary of situations too, for they inhabit the woods, rivers and skies around us. However, to catch sight of a monster is still a rare and wonderful thing; only those who truly open their eyes will be lucky enough to ever glimpse one.

## MONSTER VARIETY

Like creatures of the natural world, a monster's body features are perfectly suited to its habitat. For example, the majestic griffin – part eagle and part lion – makes its home in mountainous regions. This sure-footed beast is able to clamber nimbly over rough ground, though is equally at home soaring through the skies in search of jewels and other treasures. In Australia, the man-eating bunyip has nostrils on top of its head, allowing it to lurk just beneath the surface of swamps and creeks. This beast's long curved tusks are vital for hauling its heavy body on to dry land, as well as for "hooking" unfortunate passers-by.

This rugged mountain landscape, with its freshwater stream and wide open sky, is undoubtedly home to many fantastic beasts.

*A troll's woodland lair*

*A dragon's desert shelter*

7

These beast tracks from around the world include the clawed footprints of a baby snow dragon (bottom right) and the unmistakable jungle track of a man-eating manticore (right centre).

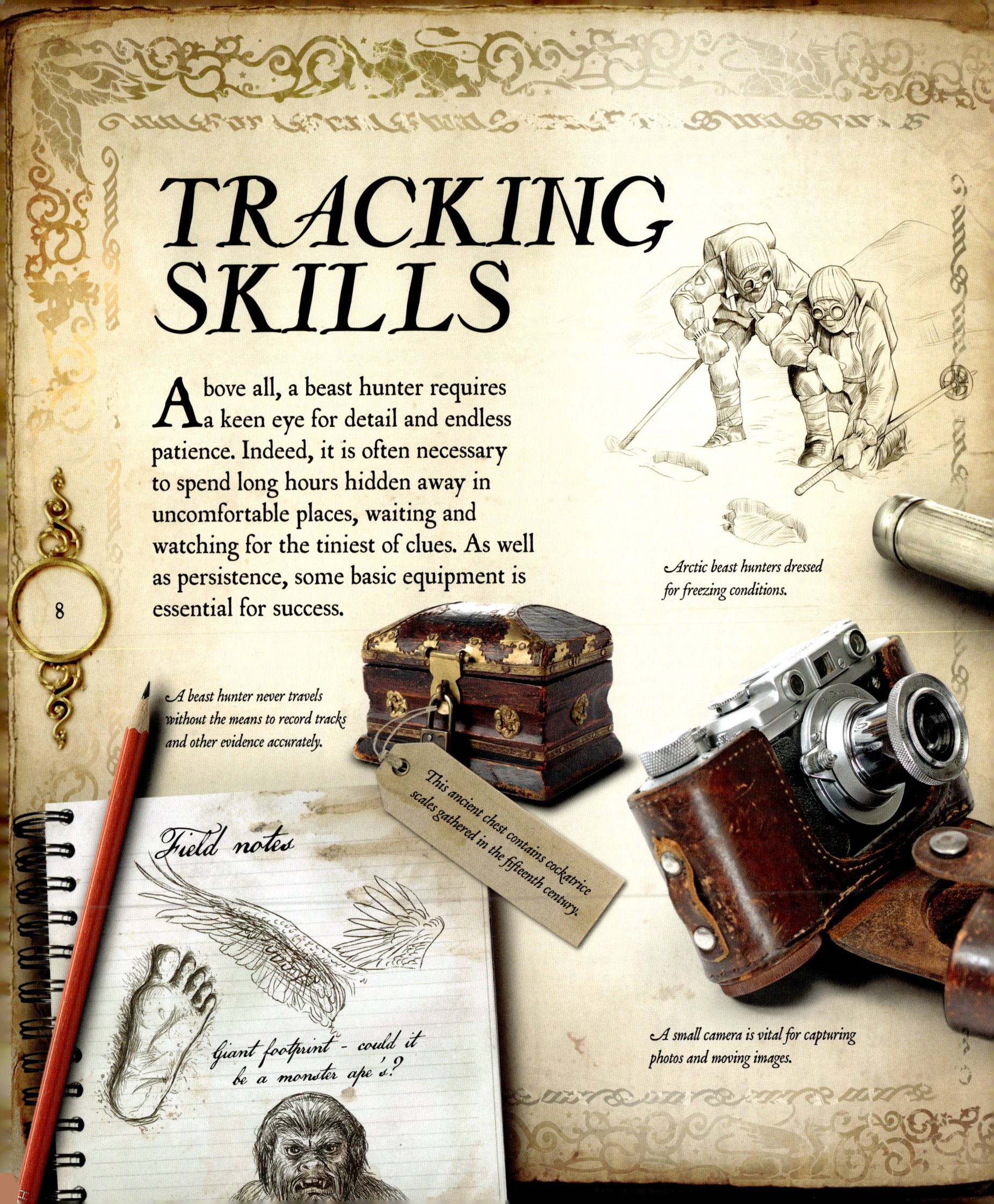

# TRACKING SKILLS

Above all, a beast hunter requires a keen eye for detail and endless patience. Indeed, it is often necessary to spend long hours hidden away in uncomfortable places, waiting and watching for the tiniest of clues. As well as persistence, some basic equipment is essential for success.

*Arctic beast hunters dressed for freezing conditions.*

*A beast hunter never travels without the means to record tracks and other evidence accurately.*

*This ancient chest contains cockatrice scales gathered in the fifteenth century.*

*Field notes*

*Giant footprint – could it be a monster ape's?*

*A small camera is vital for capturing photos and moving images.*

# MAGICAL CHARMS

Monsters rarely follow the laws of the known natural world, and it may be necessary to use tried-and-tested charms when dealing with unwelcome behaviour or attempting to lure a beast from its lair. Some of these spells will be detailed on the following pages. It is, however, advisable for beginners to learn the following ditty, which may be used to calm an angry beast:

*Binoculars are essential for viewing beasts from a safe distance.*

*Many beasts, and particularly those of a supernatural nature, are best observed under cover of darkness.*

Oh wondrous beast, pray hear this charm
I am your friend and mean no harm
Oh, stay in sight. Do not take flight!
Spare me from your claws and bite!

*Vials are required for gathering samples.*

*A jungle shelter built from sticks allows safe beast-viewing.*

*Tracking ocean-dwelling beasts requires deep-sea diving skills.*

*Jars are helpful to preserve larger specimens.*

Unidentified tentacle
Cambodia

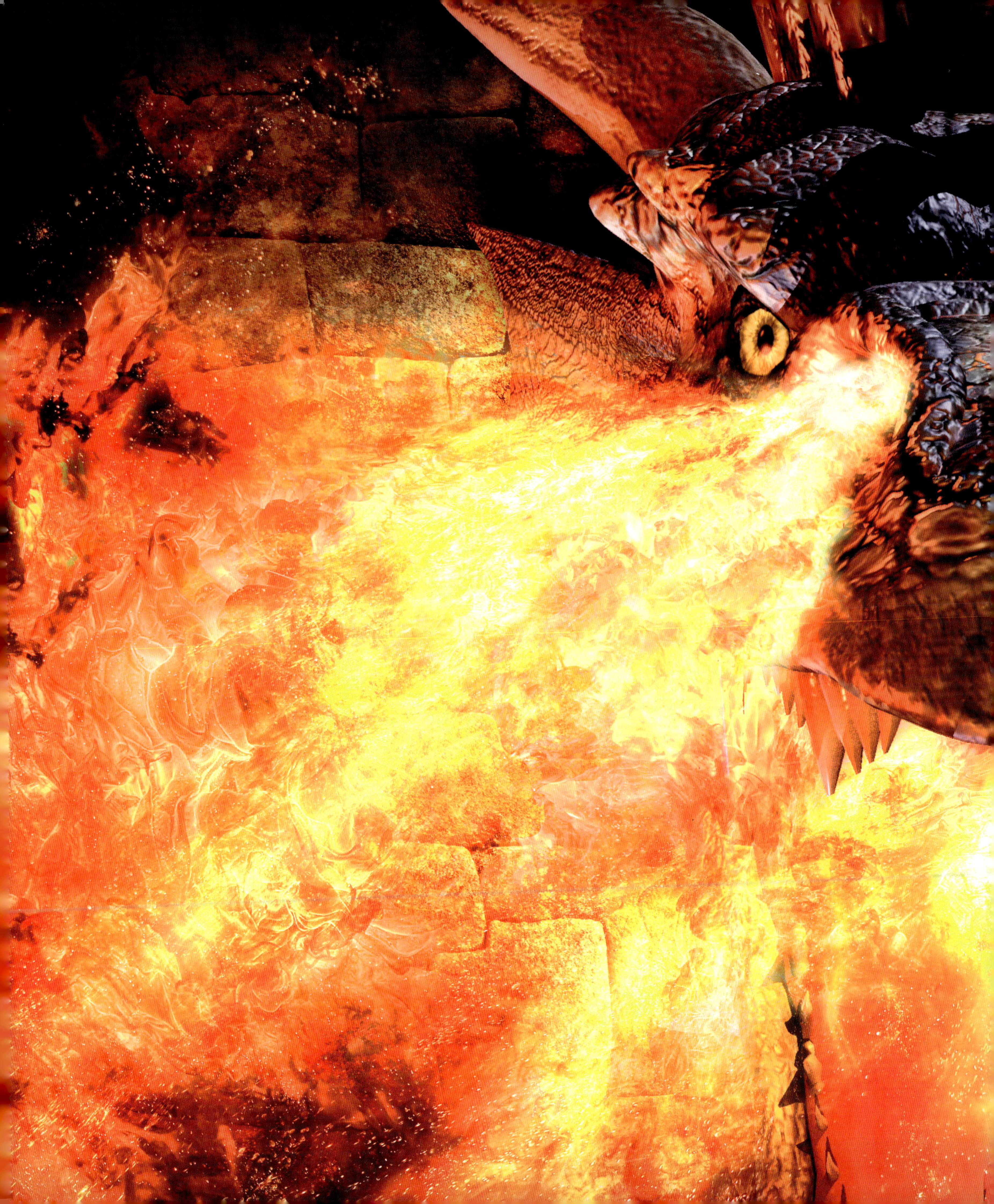

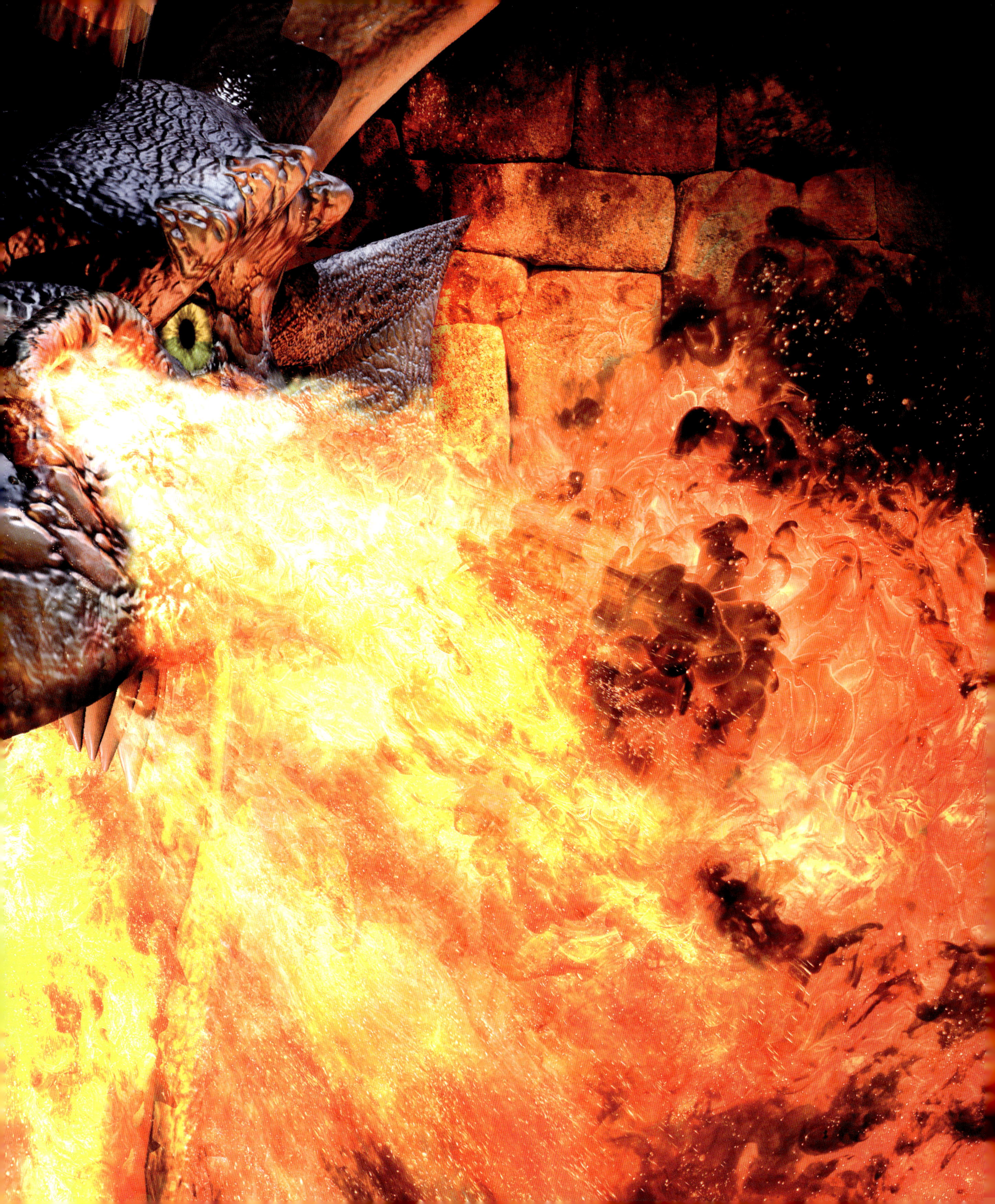

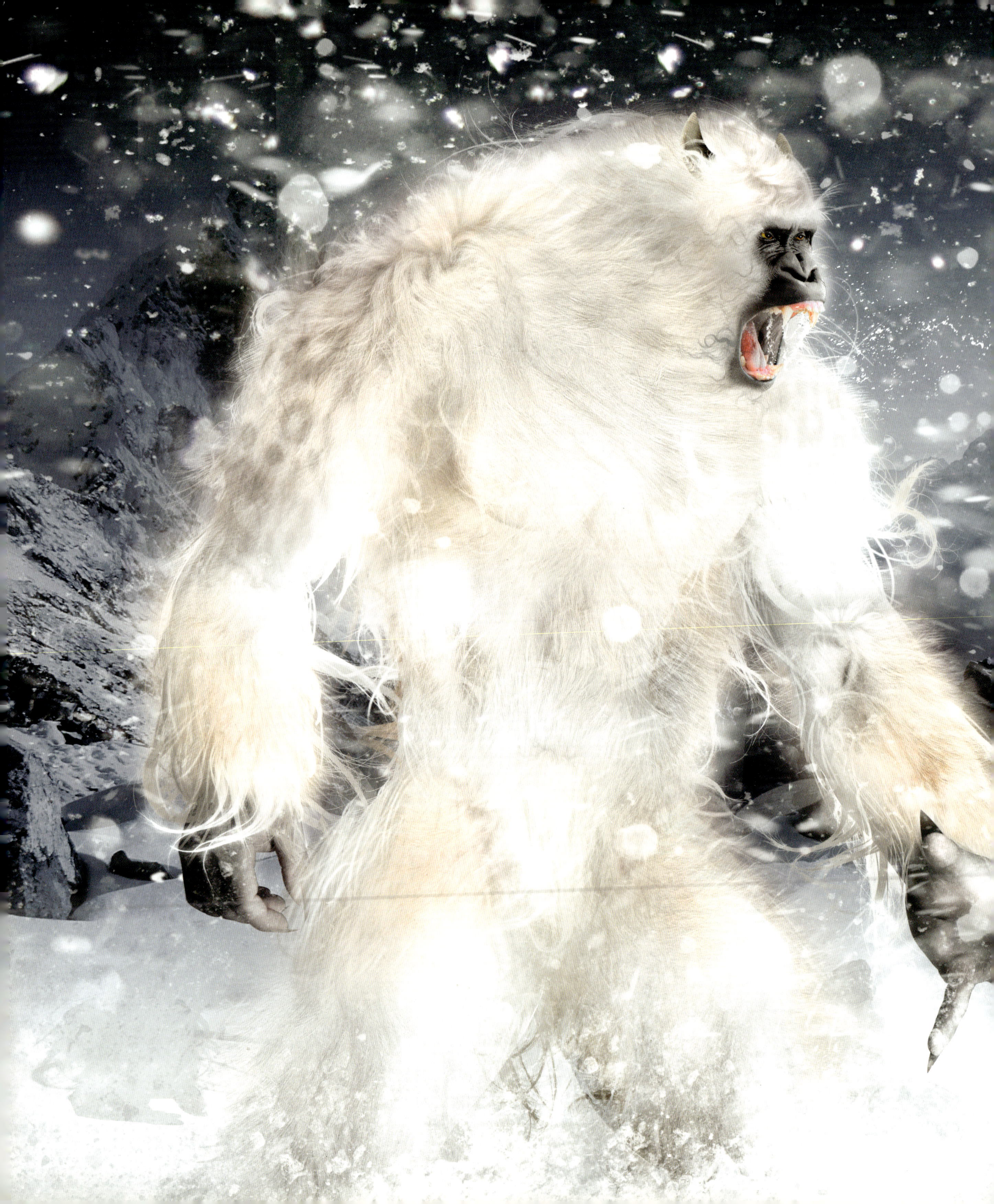

# BEASTS OF THE EARTH

FROM VAST MOUNTAIN RANGES TO DARK, SILENT FORESTS WHERE FEW WOULD EVER DARE TO TREAD, MANY STRANGE AND WONDERFUL CREATURES INHABIT THE FAR-FLUNG CORNERS OF OUR WORLD.

# MOUNTAIN AND FOREST BEASTS

A variety of beasts make their homes in dark, silent forests, or high up in mountainous regions. Tracking such monsters can prove challenging, as it requires courage and good survival skills to venture to such remote regions. Some of the hardest beasts to study are trolls, because they make their lairs in deep forest burrows or black mountain caves. These hideous creatures avoid daylight at all costs, since the sun's rays will turn them to stone. By night, trolls rampage through the wilderness in search of prey, pouncing upon any human they chance to encounter.

*Travellers exploring remote regions make easy prey for greedy trolls!*

*This massive molar found in a Canadian forest almost certainly comes from a bigfoot.*

# MONSTER APES

The vast Himalayan Mountains of Asia are home to one of the world's most mysterious monsters — the yeti. For centuries, terrified inhabitants have reported seeing giant footprints in the snow, and many claim to have glimpsed a huge, ape-like figure moving across the icy landscape. Bigfoot, a similar ape-monster, stalks the wilderness regions of North America and Canada. Although secretive in nature, this beast seems to enjoy playing tricks on humans. On the other hand, the Australian yowie avoids people at all costs, although it can be incredibly fierce if cornered.

*Fur from an Australian yowie.*

# MIGHTY GIANTS

Hideous and hulking, giants are feared for their extraordinary strength. As old as the Earth itself, some like to meddle in the affairs of man, while others - like this frost giant - are only ever glimpsed in the remote wilderness.

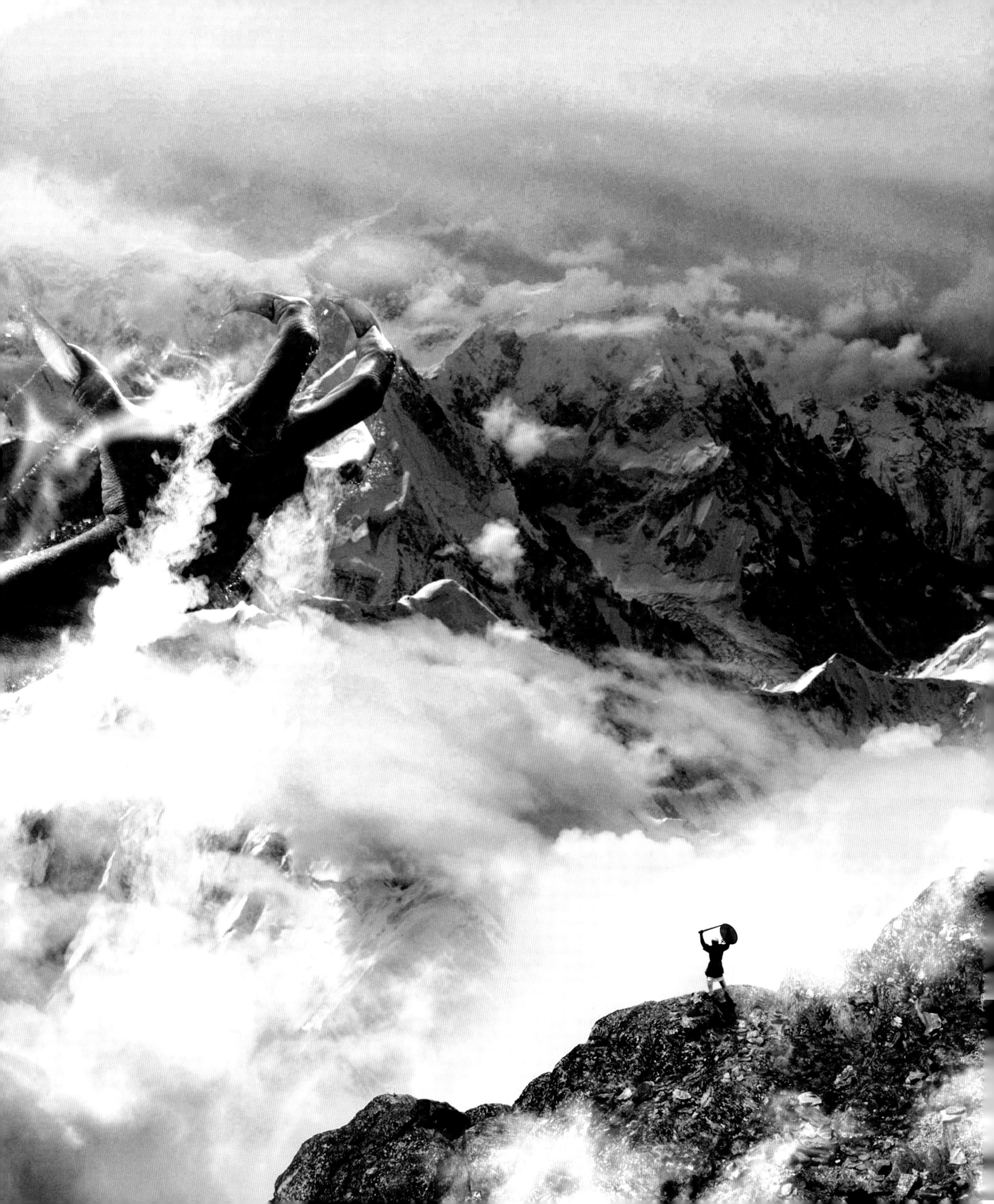

# HALF HUMANS

Many of the world's most horrifying beasts have human features. Those venturing into jungles must watch out for the man-eating manticore. With a human head, a lion's body, three rows of savage teeth and a deadly dragon's tail, this creature may briefly be mistaken for a very short man. Across southern Europe, beware of the screeching harpies! With women's faces and vultures' bodies, these clawed beasts swoop down from the skies to snatch food.

*The manticore*

*Harpy Study*

*Huge talons*

*The terrible smell that follows the harpies around serves as a warning that they are nearby.*

*Minotaur Study*

*This ancient Minotaur horn is believed to have dark magical powers.*

# PART MAN, PART BULL

The ancient Greeks told of the ferocious Minotaur, a terrifying creature that was part man, part bull. Thankfully now extinct, this bellowing monster was kept at the centre of a maze by King Minos of Crete. Every nine years, 14 young men and women were sacrificed to the beast to satisfy its craving for human flesh. Eventually, the Athenian hero Theseus ended the terror by slaying the monster in its lair.

# THE GORGONS

It was while travelling through Greece that I first had the opportunity to study those snake-haired monsters known as the Gorgons. By chance, I struck up a conversation with an old fisherman on the island of Serifos. When the man discovered my profession, he told me that he could lead me to the Gorgons' secret lair.

*Hair of venomous snakes*

*A half-serpent Gorgon*

*A pack of limbed Gorgons*

*A deadly gaze*

## A DEADLY GAZE

I was somewhat alarmed, for all monster trackers know that the Gorgons are among the most deadly of beasts. Legend tells that one glance alone from their staring eyes is enough to turn any creature to stone! However, the chance to prove their existence could not be missed, and so the following day I boarded the man's boat.

*A mouse turned to stone.*

### Vital statistics

| | |
|---|---|
| Name: | Gorgon |
| Description: | Very ugly; hypnotic eyes; serpent hair |
| Call: | Loud hissing (from hair region) |
| Diet: | Human organs |
| Behaviour: | Cunning; without mercy |

# Gorgon Study

Snake skin from the Gorgons' lair.

### 19 July, near Serifos

We are sailing west in a boat named the Medusa. My companion only smiles mysteriously when I enquire as to our whereabouts. However, he has given me a small mirror and told me that should we chance upon a Gorgon, to look only at the creature's reflection — otherwise I might meet a stony end!

### 20 July

Late this afternoon, we arrived on a rocky and seemingly deserted island. My guide led the way to a damp, eerie cave. No Gorgons appeared to be present, but I was horrified to see several figures of people and animals that had been turned to stone. I removed a mouse as evidence, as well as scraps of what appears to be snake skin.

*Snake skin has a strange glow — magical powers?*

*The Gorgons are no beauty queens!*

*A mirror is essential for the safe viewing of Gorgons.*

# CENTAURS AND SIRENS

The forest-dwelling creatures known as centaurs have the head, arms and chest of a man, and a horse's body and legs. Known for their unpredictable behaviour, these quick-witted creatures think with their human brains and must be treated with extreme caution! However, a few centaurs – like the wise Chiron of Greek myths – have risen above their beastly nature, and are gentle and civilized.

*Most centaurs are aggressive creatures, known for their wild behaviour.*

## WINGED SPHINX

The ancient Greeks told of a hideous monster called the Sphinx. This beast had a lion's body, the head of a woman, the wings of a great eagle and a serpent-headed tail. Any visitor entering the city of Thebes had to answer the Sphinx's riddle correctly, or be devoured – and countless lives were lost. However, a traveller called Oedipus was able to guess the right answer. Wild with fury, the Sphinx threw herself off a cliff, and – thankfully – has never been seen again.

*A Greek relief showing Oedipus and the Sphinx.*

## THE SPHINX'S RIDDLE

What has four legs in the morning, two legs in the afternoon and three legs in the evening?

Answer: Man – as a baby, he crawls on all fours; as an adult, he walks upright on two legs; and as an old man, he walks with the aid of a stick.

## THE SIRENS

On islands dotted throughout the oceans live the bewitching Sirens. With the upper bodies of women and the lower bodies of birds, they appear rather beautiful at first glance. Beware, however, for their pretty faces hide vicious teeth! Many sailors have been lured to their deaths by their spellbinding singing, a sound that is almost impossible to resist.

*The ancient Greek hero Odysseus encountered the Sirens on his journey back from the Trojan Wars.*

# DEADLY SPIDER WEBS

Monstrous spiders lurk at the heart of dark, enchanted forests. Emerging from the shadows by night, they spin shimmering webs of gold and silver to ensnare careless travellers. Their silk is so strong, that even the sharpest sword cannot cut through it.

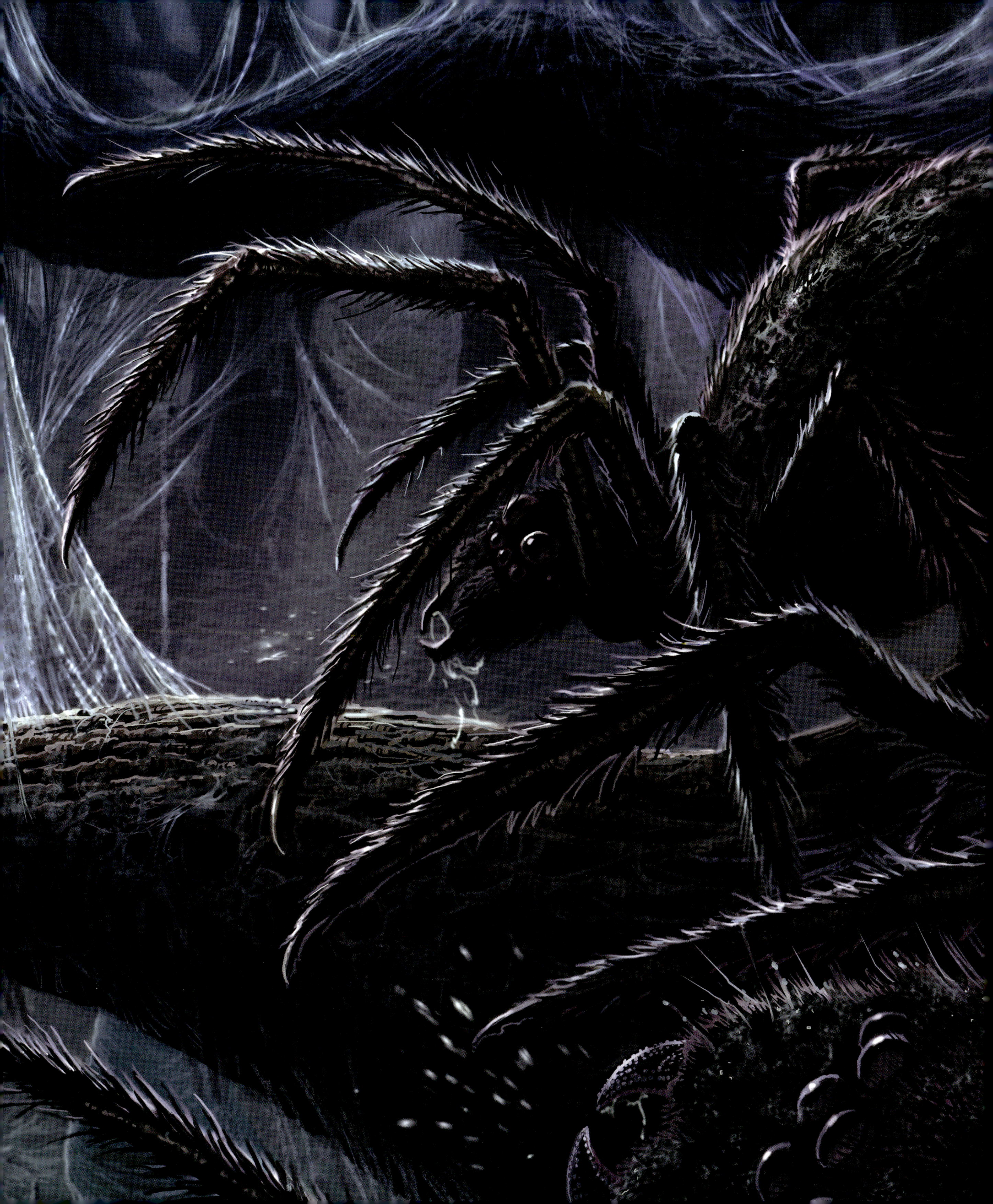

# CERBERUS

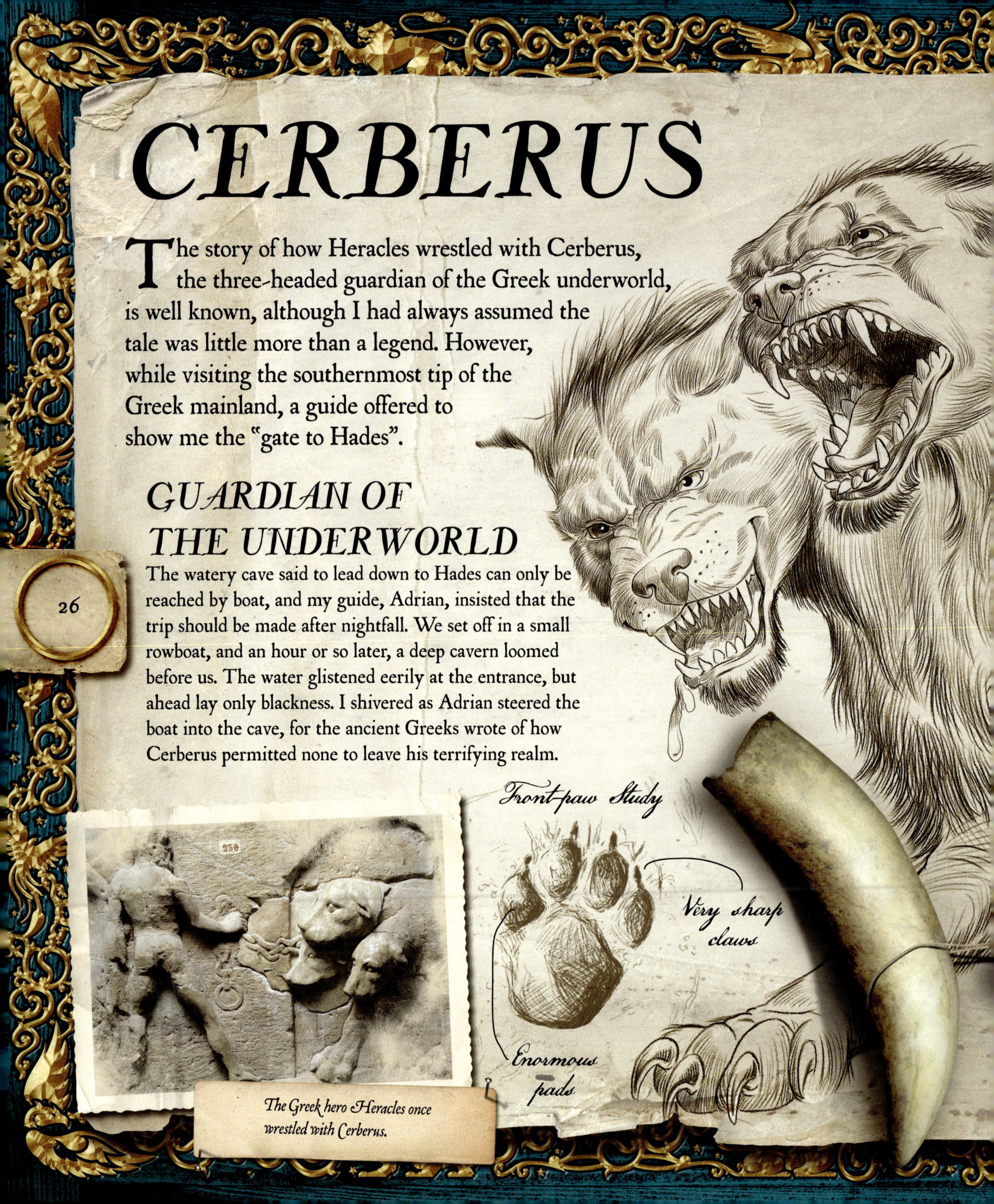

The story of how Heracles wrestled with Cerberus, the three-headed guardian of the Greek underworld, is well known, although I had always assumed the tale was little more than a legend. However, while visiting the southernmost tip of the Greek mainland, a guide offered to show me the "gate to Hades".

## GUARDIAN OF THE UNDERWORLD

The watery cave said to lead down to Hades can only be reached by boat, and my guide, Adrian, insisted that the trip should be made after nightfall. We set off in a small rowboat, and an hour or so later, a deep cavern loomed before us. The water glistened eerily at the entrance, but ahead lay only blackness. I shivered as Adrian steered the boat into the cave, for the ancient Greeks wrote of how Cerberus permitted none to leave his terrifying realm.

*Front-paw Study*

*Very sharp claws*

*Enormous pads*

*The Greek hero Heracles once wrestled with Cerberus.*

# Cerberus Study

## Vital statistics

| | |
|---|---|
| Name: | Cerberus |
| Description: | Three-headed hound; glowing red eyes |
| Call: | Spine-chilling barks and snarls |
| Diet: | Passing strangers |
| Behaviour: | Ever-watchful; prone to gnashing teeth |

*A ferocious bite*

*A massive fang found at the cave entrance.*

Each of Cerberus's three savage heads will feed only on living meat.

### 21 January, Cape Tainaron, Greece

After a few moments, Adrian stopped rowing and pointed to a large opening in the rock face ahead. Silently, I clambered from the vessel and swiftly gathered evidence. Once I was safely back in the boat, Adrian uttered the following words in a commanding voice:

Oh, Hound of Hades, your lair is found
Where dead souls enter underground.

From just above our heads came a ferocious snarl and a terrible gnashing of teeth. It was clear that we were in mortal danger. Adrian began to row away quickly. I forced myself to glance back — and saw six red eyes burning through the blackness.

# GOBLINS AND DWARFS

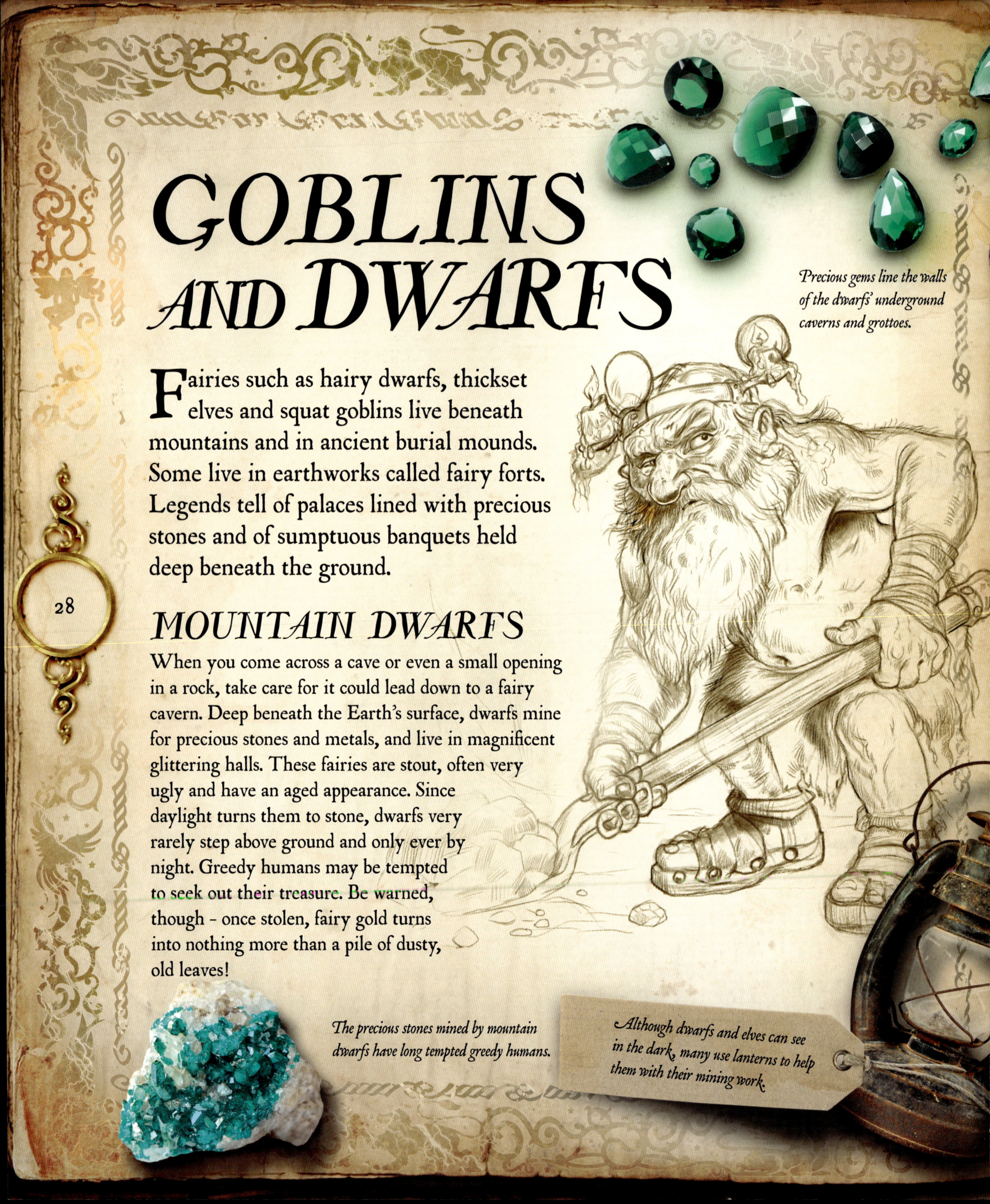

*Precious gems line the walls of the dwarfs' underground caverns and grottoes.*

Fairies such as hairy dwarfs, thickset elves and squat goblins live beneath mountains and in ancient burial mounds. Some live in earthworks called fairy forts. Legends tell of palaces lined with precious stones and of sumptuous banquets held deep beneath the ground.

## MOUNTAIN DWARFS

When you come across a cave or even a small opening in a rock, take care for it could lead down to a fairy cavern. Deep beneath the Earth's surface, dwarfs mine for precious stones and metals, and live in magnificent glittering halls. These fairies are stout, often very ugly and have an aged appearance. Since daylight turns them to stone, dwarfs very rarely step above ground and only ever by night. Greedy humans may be tempted to seek out their treasure. Be warned, though – once stolen, fairy gold turns into nothing more than a pile of dusty, old leaves!

*The precious stones mined by mountain dwarfs have long tempted greedy humans.*

*Although dwarfs and elves can see in the dark, many use lanterns to help them with their mining work.*

*Any human that accepts a drink from a fairy goblet is in grave danger of enchantment.*

# FAIRY FEASTS

Walk nine times around a fairy fort on a full moon and you could find yourself a guest at a fairy banquet. In splendid dining halls, fairy folk feast from plates piled high with tempting delicacies and drink from jewel-studded goblets. If you are offered food or wine, however, turn it down at all costs! People who partake in such a feast will instantly see that the delicious food is no more than slugs and snails, and the glittering palace but a dull hole in the ground. Worst of all, though, it is almost impossible for enchanted humans to return to where they came from.

# MINIATURE MINERS

Knockers make their homes in mines and ancient quarries. These tiny workers can be extremely helpful, and the sounds of their tiny pickaxes have been known to lead people to rich pockets of silver and gold. Although largely peaceful, knockers are driven into furious rages by the sound of humans whistling.

*The tinny sounds of miniature pickaxes beneath ground are a sure sign that knockers are at work.*

# HELPFUL ELVES

Fairies that move into people's homes can be extremely helpful. Nimble-fingered elves will sew or make shoes for the whole family, while other sprites enjoy sweeping and dusting. Beware of taking a fairy's help for granted though – humans who do not leave out tasty treats may be awoken at night by a clammy hand or find stones in their shoes.

## MINIATURE HOUSEKEEPERS

Brownies have flat faces and shaggy brown hair, and wear tattered old clothes. Despite their dishevelled appearance, these tiny fairies cannot abide a messy house – while humans sleep, they pick up toys, wash dishes and even iron clothes. In return, they expect to be given a bowl of creamy milk and something to satisfy their sweet tooth – fudge is a firm favourite. Brownies are extremely proud creatures, however. If you tried to give one a new set of clothes, for example, he would be likely to move out immediately.

*Industrious elves are well known for their skill as shoemakers. Beware of taking their gifts for granted, though!*

# THE LOYAL DOMOVOI

This hardworking elf can make a household run very smoothly, and will always wake the family with loud groans if danger threatens. The domovoi usually makes his lair behind the oven or up in the attic. He is very rarely seen, though unexplained scratching noises or light footsteps may signal his presence. This fairy sheds and renews his wrinkled skin on 30 March every year, and will be very bad-tempered as a result. Always provide extra fairy treats on this day, and make an effort to help him keep your house spick and span!

*House elves appreciate offerings of sweet treats in return for their help with household chores.*

# BEASTS of the EARTH

## RARE SPECIMENS

*a collection of*
TEETH, CLAWS and OTHER CURIOSITIES
*discovered on expeditions
to the far-flung corners of the Earth*

ABOVE *This giant troll tooth was found near human remains in a deep forest-burrow.*

ABOVE *Scaly skin taken from the dragon-like tail of the deadly manticore.*

ABOVE *Found on a frozen mountain peak, this fang is almost certainly a frost giant's.*

**LEFT** *This hooked harpy claw, discovered in Greece, is the only known specimen of its kind.*

**LEFT** *This clump of bigfoot fur was discovered caught on tree bark at Bluff Creek, California.*

**ABOVE** *This yowie claw is kept in a sealed chest. Any who touch it are likely to have bad fortune.*

**RIGHT** *A piece of horn from the chimera's goat-like head.*

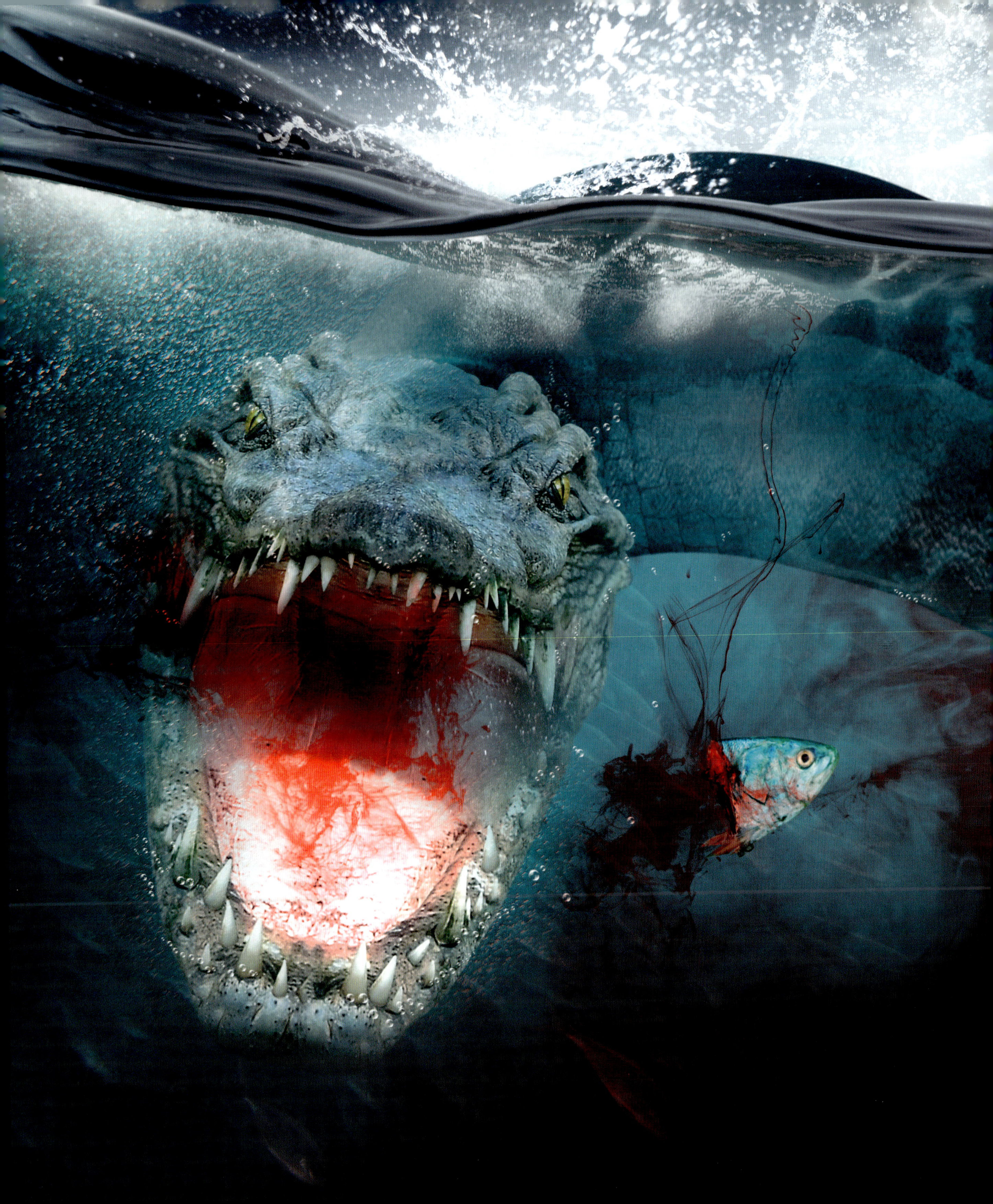

# WATER MONSTERS

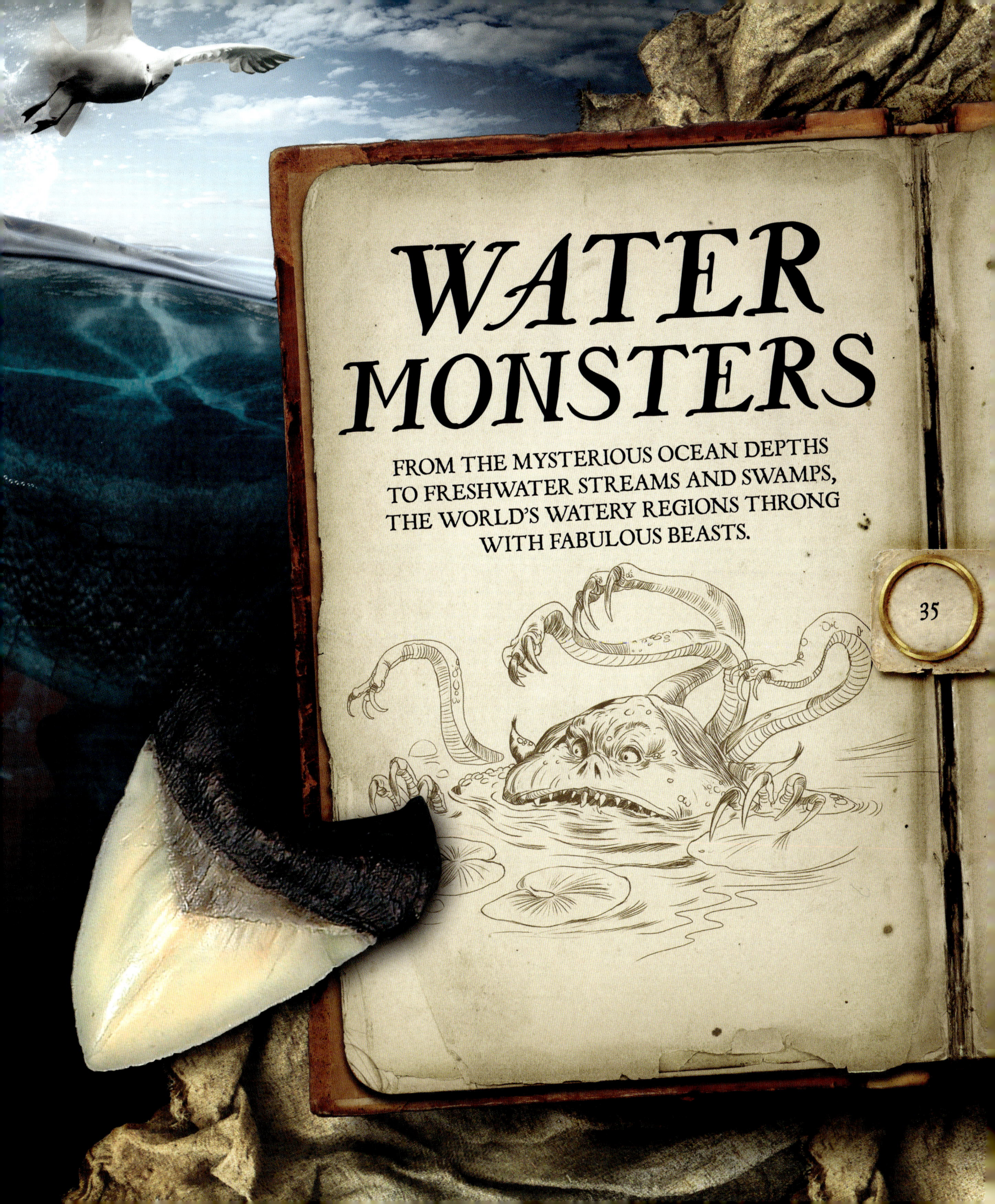

FROM THE MYSTERIOUS OCEAN DEPTHS TO FRESHWATER STREAMS AND SWAMPS, THE WORLD'S WATERY REGIONS THRONG WITH FABULOUS BEASTS.

# WATER SERPENTS

The scourge of seas and freshwater lakes, powerful water serpents lurk within many seemingly calm waters. With massively long bodies, these beasts possess gaping jaws lined with razor-sharp teeth. Most move like land snakes, though some have paddle-like limbs. When excitable, these creatures are capable of creating enormous waves, though they are known for the sneaky manner in which they can slide through water creating barely a ripple. Passing boats and unsuspecting swimmers are sucked swiftly down and usually consumed whole.

## WAITING AND WATCHING

It is often said that water serpents are "shy" due to their habit of staying hidden from view, though "cunning" is probably a better description. Indeed, these creatures are capable of lying motionless for hours at a time, and may be mistaken for floating logs. An exception to this is the sea serpent of Cape Ann, Massachusetts, in North America, which hundreds have claimed to have seen over the years. On the other hand, the Loch Ness Monster of Scotland has been witnessed much less frequently and appears to be most active late at night.

*A jagged lake-serpent tooth found washed ashore.*

*Poisonous barbs are found on the tails of some species.*

The Southern Ocean is home to a rare and deadly sea serpent with a lion-like head.

37

# THE MIDGARD SERPENT

IN VIKING MYTHS, the god Loki had three monstrous children: the giant wolf Fenrir, the dreadful goddess Hel, and Jormungand, a giant serpent also known as the Midgard Serpent. Even the gods were afraid of this horrifying creature, and the chief god Odin tossed it into the ocean. Although there have been no sightings for a very long time, some say the serpent still lurks beneath the waves, waiting to rise up from the depths and crush passing ships in its massive jaws.

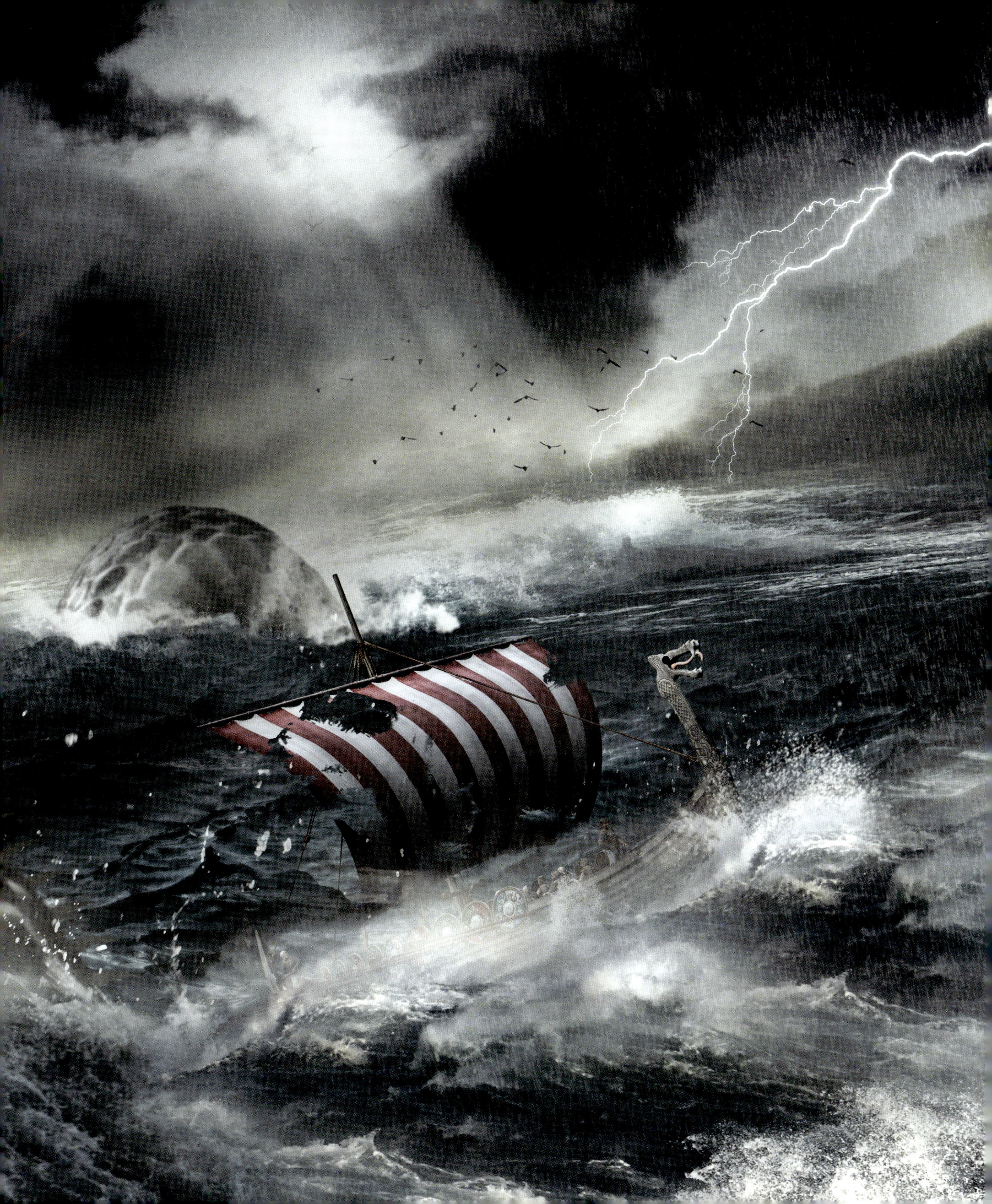

# THE KRAKEN

Of all the terrifying beasts that hide beneath the waves, it is the kraken that fills me with most dread. This squid-like monster is so enormous that some unfortunate souls have mistaken its vast body for an island. When the time came to make a proper study of this creature, I realized I must turn to the ancient wisdom of the great monster hunters for guidance.

*Kraken Study*

## GRASPING TENTACLES

Before my crew and I set sail in our research vessel, the "Hippocamp", I carefully studied the many stories of ships being dragged down by the kraken's enormous tentacles. However, some experts claimed that the monster actually preferred eating other sea monsters to humans. It was only if a ship happened to be passing that the vessel - and its crew - would be sucked down and consumed.

*Krakens only rise from the icy depths to feed.*

*The kraken's immense tentacles are strong enough to sink ships.*

It has been observed that krakens are only ever found in waters more than 80 fathoms deep. If a depth reading suddenly and inexplicably falls below 30 fathoms, then you may assume – with some certainty – that a kraken is lurking beneath your vessel!

*Muscular tongue*

*An extract from Fantastic Beasts of the Seven Seas by Professor A. Koken*

## Vital statistics

Name: The kraken
Description: Squid-like; massively long tentacles
Call: Mournful wails
Diet: Sea serpents; whales; people (in order of preference)
Behaviour: High and mighty; inconsiderate

*Eight massively long tentacles are lined with powerful "suckers".*

# A GIANT WHIRLPOOL

After several months at sea, we found ourselves just off the coast of Iceland. One still afternoon, the sea's depth reading suddenly plummeted and I realized we might be in grave peril. Sailing rapidly south, we anchored at what we hoped was a safe distance and anxiously waited. Soon, the sea began to toss and swell, and a giant, slimy mass broke through the waves. Massive, writhing tentacles stretched out from the body, grasping for prey and almost reaching our vessel. Then, this incredible "island" sank from sight, and with it millions of fish - as well as some larger unidentified creatures - were sucked down into a raging whirlpool.

*The suckers trap prey.*

41

# FRESHWATER BEASTS

The rivers, lakes and swamps of the world are home to a startling variety of fearsome beasts. Small children and animals that stray too near to the water's edge are at particular risk from some of these creatures. However, all must take care, for it is a sad fact that many adults have vanished in mysterious circumstances while taking a riverside stroll or going for a quick swim.

*Bunyip Study*

*Bunyip tusk*

## LYING IN WAIT

Hidden beneath bridges or submerged just below the water's surface, hideous water trolls lie in wait for their prey. These creatures are always hungry and will snatch victims at every opportunity. The less common gryndylow is found in bogs or lakes, and occasionally even in garden ponds. This fearsome little creature uses octopus-like tentacles to grasp its prey. In Australia, the terrible man-eating bunyip hides out in swamps and creeks. Although hardly ever seen, this beast's presence is certainly felt at night when its blood-curdling howls may be heard from a great distance.

*Very few have seen the bunyip and lived to tell the tale.*

## Gryndylow Study

Exceptional eyesight

Tentacles can sense the tiniest movement.

## Kelpie Study

## THE KELPIE

The mysterious kelpie is a beautiful horse seen wandering along the banks of rivers and lakes. The creature appears to be lost, and many have made the mistake of mounting its sleek back, for this gentle-eyed horse nuzzles those who approach it. However, any who attempt to ride it are doomed, for they become stuck fast and cannot escape. The kelpie then gallops off at speed and plunges into deep water, carrying its unfortunate victim down to a silent grave.

The kelpie's gentle appearance hides a dark nature.

A kelpie's hoof print.

# SELKIE

If you look out to sea at the bobbing head of a seal, you may notice eerily human eyes gazing back at you. Selkies are seals that have the ability to transform into fairy maidens. On Midsummer's Eve, they throw off their magical skins and come ashore to dance. Any selkie that loses its skin, however, will be doomed to remain on land.

A few years ago, I received the following letter from the Scottish island of Orkney:

> Some years ago, I did a terrible thing. It was a warm night and, unable to sleep, I came down to the beach. Several seals came ashore and I was astonished to see them transform into young women. I had grown up hearing the selkie legends and so - on impulse - I took one of their discarded skins and waited to see what would happen. When the women came back, all but one picked up their skins and returned to the sea. The last was distraught and disappeared on foot.

## MAGICAL SKIN

When we finally spoke, the man told me he had hidden the sealskin away and forgotten it. However, he had recently heard talk of a mysterious woman who was said to haunt the shoreline at night. He had decided he would leave the sealskin out where he had found it; having heard of my fairy research, he invited me to watch.

*Before the selkie disappeared, she dropped this shell. Listen closely and you can hear the murmur of distant shores...*

*If a selkie maiden loses her precious sealskin, she can never return to the sea.*

### 23 June, Orkney, Scotland

Last night we hid behind a sand dune. After midnight, a woman appeared in the distance. Her face was shadowed, but as she drew near it became clear she was weeping. Then her gaze fell upon the sealskin — in delight she threw it over her shoulders and before our very eyes seemed to melt away. Seconds later, the sleek head of a seal popped up above the water — it turned for a moment to look at us, and then dived beneath the waves.

### Vital statistics

Name: Selkie
Description: Either a seal or a beautiful maiden
Call: Sings sweetly
Diet: In seal form, fish; in maiden form may struggle to adapt to human diet
Behaviour: Delights in moonlight dancing; frequently breaks human hearts

## WATER MONSTERS

# RARE SPECIMENS

*A collection of* TEETH, TUSKS and OTHER CURIOSITIES *found on expeditions to the world's watery regions*

**ABOVE** *A shark-like tooth found washed up on the shore of Loch Ness in Scotland.*

**RIGHT** *Horned sea monsters are a rare but deadly presence in the world's oceans.*

**ABOVE** *The bunyip uses its curved tusks to heave itself on to dry land and "hook" passers-by.*

**LEFT** *This skin fragment from an unidentified sea monster is tougher than a rhinoceros hide.*

**RIGHT** *The serrated tooth of a water serpent encountered in the icy depths of the Arctic Ocean.*

**ABOVE** *The enlarged eyes of the gryndylow allow this beast to detect prey in very dark water.*

**RIGHT** *A tentacle segment, cut from a huge sea beast as it attempted to drag down a boat.*

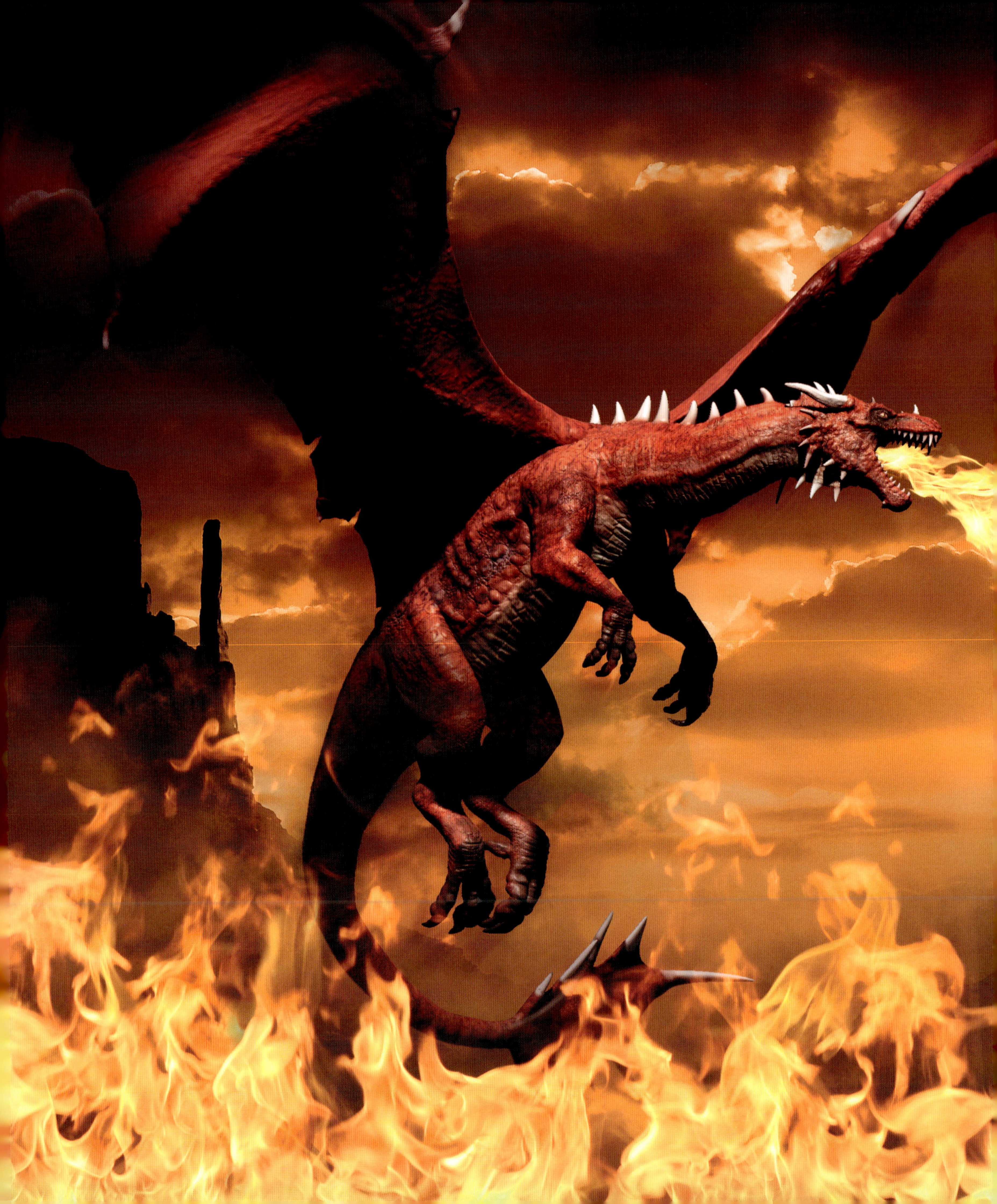

# BEASTS OF THE AIR

THE SKIES ABOVE US ARE HOME TO A MULTITUDE OF WINGED WONDERS, FROM MAJESTIC BIRD-BEASTS TO FIRE-BREATHING DRAGONS.

# DRAGONS

*Dragon Study*

Ferocious, cunning and wise, dragons are amongst the mightiest of beasts. Some soar majestically through the skies, while others slither serpent-like through rivers and lakes. Rare dragons may be found in the most extreme places – volcanic dragons lay their eggs in bubbling lava, while snow dragons make their lairs in frozen ice caves.

*Wings are thin yet amazingly strong*

## DRAGON FIRE

As well as having dagger-sharp fangs and claws strong enough to cut through diamonds, most dragons possess the extraordinary ability to breathe scorching flames of fire. A single blast almost always results in instant death for the victim. For this reason, only experienced monster hunters should ever attempt to track dragons.

## MAGIC AND MYSTERY

Many parts of the dragon are known to possess powerful magic. Those brave enough to consume a dead dragon's heart will find this feast gives them the ability to see into the future, while eating a dragon's enormous tongue can bring great wisdom. Ground horns and bones can be used to cure various illnesses, while dragon scales may bring good luck in the right hands. The most powerful part of a dragon, though, is its blood. Wizards will go to great lengths to find this incredible substance for their spells.

*Skin is often extremely gnarled in appearance*

Dragon fire may be bottled by experienced beast hunters.

Almost all lairs have a treasure hoard

It takes hundreds of years to reach adulthood

51

Aged dragons have incredible wisdom

Of dragon blood I thee implore
To heed these words from ancient lore.
Drink it, and you will fathom the speech of birds.
But spill it, and you will lose the power of words.
Treasure it, and you will find the dragon's hoard
But lose it, and you will perish by the sword.

# DRAGON GALLERY

*A STUDY OF SPECIES*

So diverse and numerous are dragon species, that it would be impossible to name and describe them all on these pages. Shown here are six dragons from different habitats to represent the dazzling variety found amongst dragonkind.

*THE SNAGGLE-TOOTHED MOUNTAIN DRAGON* makes its lair at high altitudes in central and eastern Europe. Like all mountain species, this dragon has extraordinary eyesight, and is distinguished by a curious misalignment of its front teeth, which are nevertheless horribly vicious in attack.

*THE RAZOR-FANGED MARSH DRAGON* is found principally in southern Asia and is an ever-present threat to passing birds, mammals such as deer and buffalo, and even humans. This species cannot fly, but is surprisingly nimble on dry land.

**THE FIVE-CLAWED SERPENT DRAGON** dwells in the rivers and lakes of eastern Asia. This species is wingless, but can rise to the clouds with the aid of a discreet lump on top of its head. Possessed with a remarkable intelligence, this dragon is known to transform into many guises.

**THE PYGMY FOREST DRAGON** lives deep in the temperate forests of America and Canada. Although no bigger than an antelope, this agile and muscular dragon includes bears and mountain lions in its diet.

**THE CRYSTAL ICE DRAGON** makes its home in the snowy polar lands. Pearl-like and almost translucent in appearance, this magnificent creature soars through the skies and breathes out blasts of icy air to stun its prey of polar bears, musk oxen and moose.

**THE HORNED NIGHT DRAGON** is a relatively rare species found on the open rangelands of Australia. Notable for its spine-chilling wolf-like howl, this dragon leaves its lair only when darkness falls.

# GLACIER CAVE OF THE ANTARCTIC SNOW DRAGON

This magnificent creature has only rarely been seen by human eyes. Found at the heart of Antarctica, it spends days at a time in its icy lair during the long, harsh winter. When hungry, this dragon emerges to circle over the Antarctic sea, plunging into its freezing depths to capture giant squids, orcas and large seals.

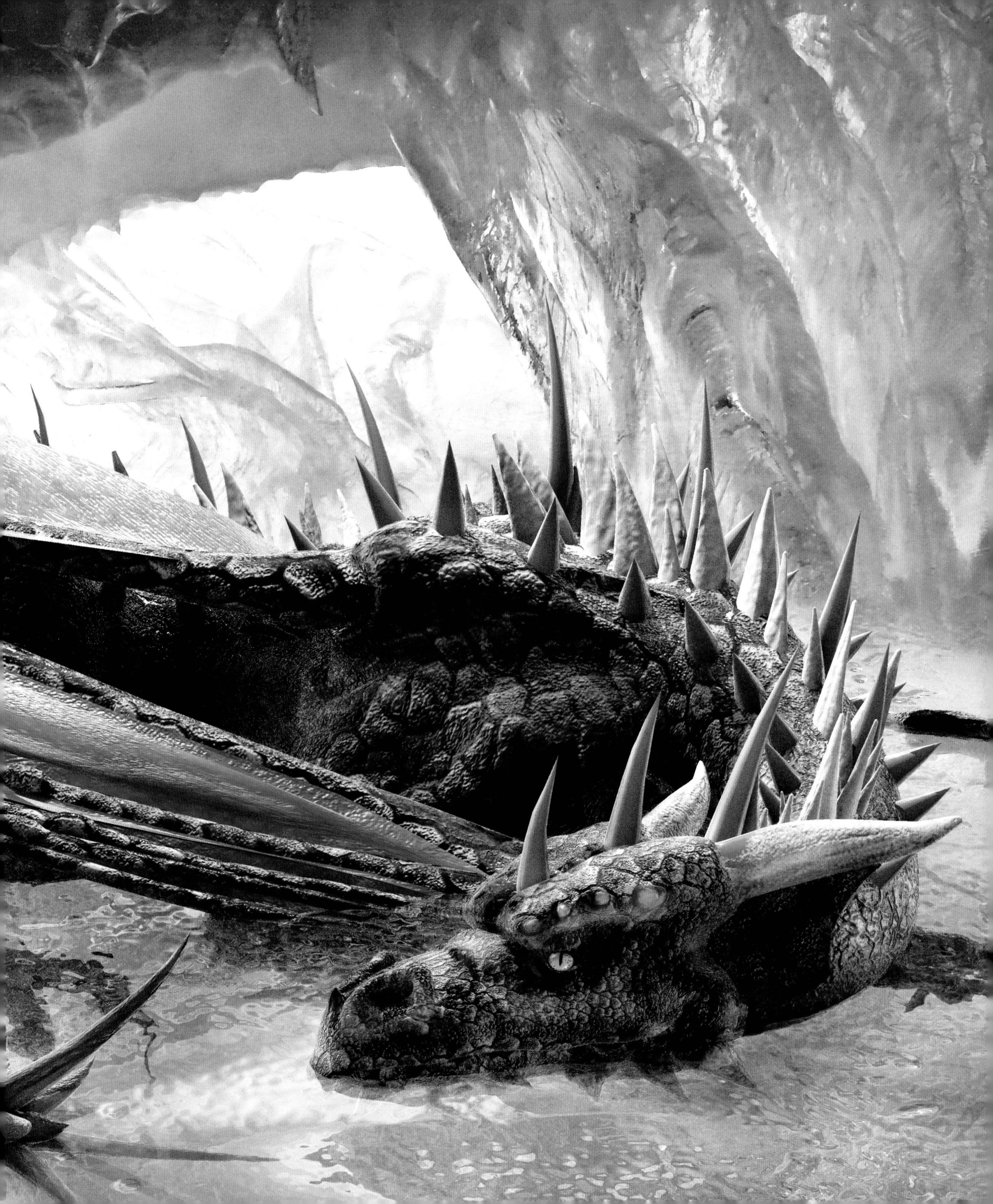

# The Sumatran Egg Collection

*Very closely guarded on Sumatra, "The Island of Gold", the six dragon eggs of this curious collection are known to make a gentle humming sound when gathered together in one place.*

1. Arabian Sand Dragon
2. Krakatoan Lava Dragon
3. Sumatran Water Dragon
4. Horned Night Dragon
5. Antarctic Snow Dragon
6. Bearded Mountain Dragon

1.

4.

2.

3.

5.

6.

# HALF BIRD, HALF BEAST

*Reptile scales start to appear underneath the neck feathers*

The skies throng with a host of incredible bird-beasts. Since they are so seldom seen by human eyes, it is thought that these creatures somehow occupy a different realm – one that only occasionally merges with the world we see.

*Cockatrice Study*

## TERRIFYING BIRD-MONSTERS

The giant griffin has the head, wings and talons of an eagle, and the hindquarters of a lion. This powerful creature is well known for its habit of stealing gold and precious stones, and guarding such treasures in its mountain nest. In Africa, the much-feared roc glides over the open plains in search of prey. Elephants are the roc's first choice of food, though it will readily swoop down to snatch other large creatures, including humans.

*Rooster wings are combined with fearsome clawed "hands"*

*Griffin*

# THE COCKATRICE

A few years ago, I happened to meet the well-known scientist Dr da'Costa, who was carrying out research on European toads. When he told me that one of the reptiles under his watch had been behaving very oddly — in short, guarding a large egg from an unknown creature — I immediately guessed that the egg might contain a deadly cockatrice. As all monster hunters know, this rare beast is the product of a cockerel's egg laid on the stroke of midnight, then incubated by a toad or serpent.

*Dragon tail*

The egg must be tended by a toad or snake before it can hatch.

*Avoid beast's eyes at all costs!*

### 14 June, Black Craw Woods
Since the toad has been guarding the egg for many months, I feel sure the cockatrice may hatch at any moment. I carry a small mirror for turning the beast's deadly gaze back upon itself, and a caged weasel. This animal is the cockatrice's sworn enemy and should protect me.

### 23 June
When I came to look at the egg this morning, the toad was hopping excitedly about. The shell began to crack and a truly extraordinary creature wriggled free. I can only describe it as half rooster, half reptile. I stayed well out of its sight, though the toad was not so lucky for the poor animal fell over stone dead.

*Must find a way to bottle the beast's scorching breath...*

# THE HIPPOGRIFF

The majestic hippogriff is the offspring of a griffin and a horse. Since griffins and horses are sworn enemies, the hippogriff is a rare beast indeed. Although I have been fortunate enough to witness griffins on several occasions, perhaps more than anything, I longed to lay eyes on a hippogriff.

## A RARE DISCOVERY

A few years ago, I spent several months studying the nesting habits of North African griffins. One afternoon, I scrambled up a steep gully to examine a nest. Expecting to see several griffin eggs and perhaps some jewels, I was instead amazed to find a single golden egg. With great excitement, I realized it must surely contain a baby hippogriff.

*Head is that of a great eagle, both cruel and majestic*

*Sleek and sturdy horse's body*

*Hooked beak for ripping through prey*

*Hind legs have a powerful kick*

*A truly majestic sight!*

*Could a hippogriff ever be tamed?*

**17 October**
Today, I finally witnessed the incredible sight of a young hippogriff as it took its maiden flight. What a marvellous creature it is!

**12 November**
The hippogriff frequently prowls the mountains alone, and I am tracking it daily. I believe it is slowly getting used to my presence, although it sometimes seems startled to see me and swiftly takes to the skies.

**18 November**
Today, the hippogriff took from my outstretched hand the gift of a dead rabbit. I am beginning to dream that in time it might actually allow me to mount its back...

# Hippogriff Study

## Vital statistics

**Name:** Hippogriff
**Description:** Part horse, part eagle; massive talons; glowing eyes
**Call:** Loud squawks; may whinny
**Diet:** Small mammals; grazes on grass
**Behaviour:** Noble; loyal; may attack if startled

*Hippogriff talon*

*Talons may reach half a metre in length*

*Immensely strong wings*

*Hippogriff feather*

## LIGHTNING SPEED

For a few weeks, I brought the hippogriff daily gifts of rabbits or mice. On one such occasion, the beast suddenly knelt down as if to encourage me to climb onto its back. Although much afraid, I grasped its feathered neck and pulled myself up. The hippogriff began to gallop, and then in a flash we were soaring over mountains at lightning speed. It is hard to describe the experience now, for it seemed like a dream. Indeed, perhaps I might believe it was a dream, but for the fact that I still have a beautiful feather that came away in my hand.

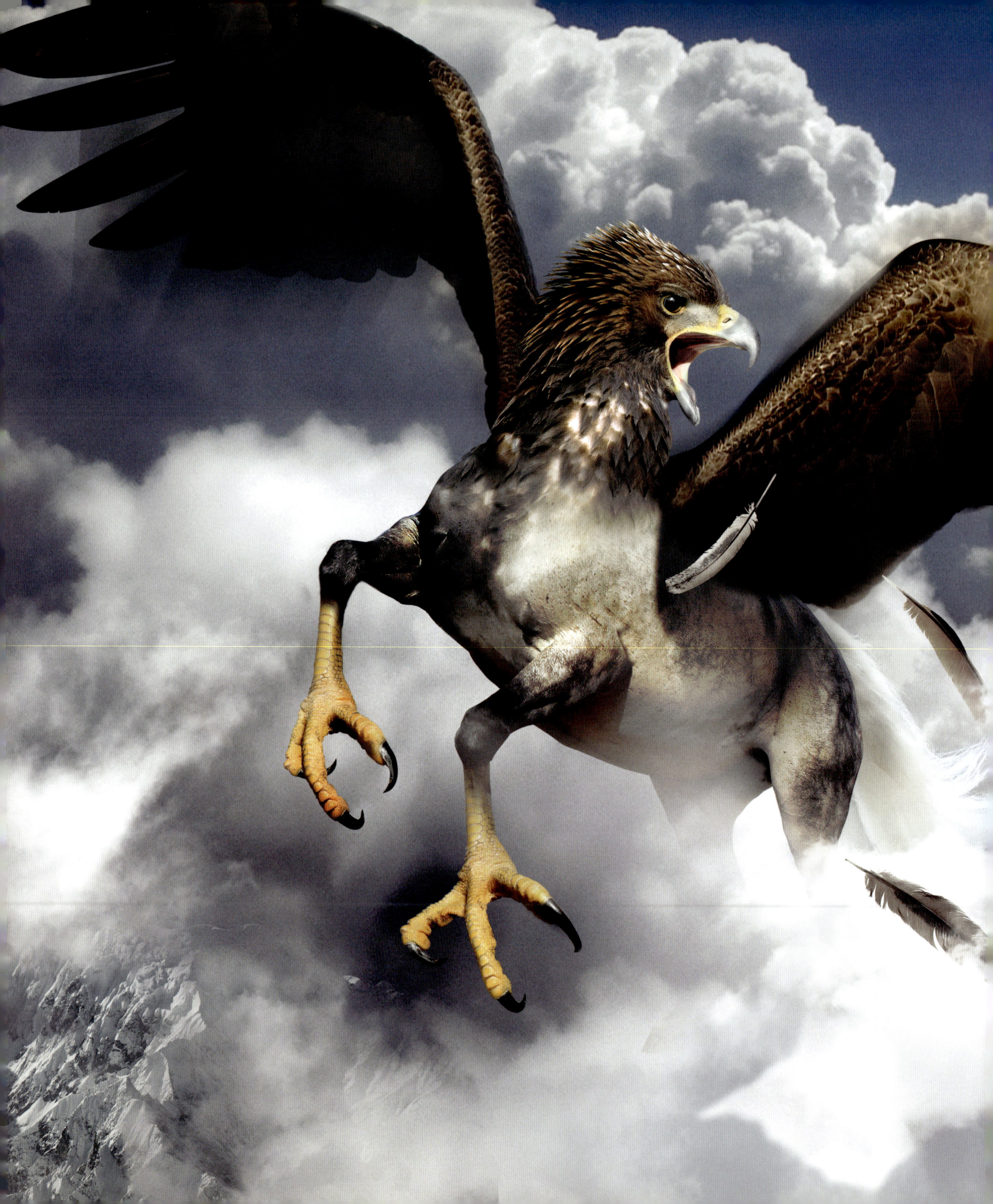

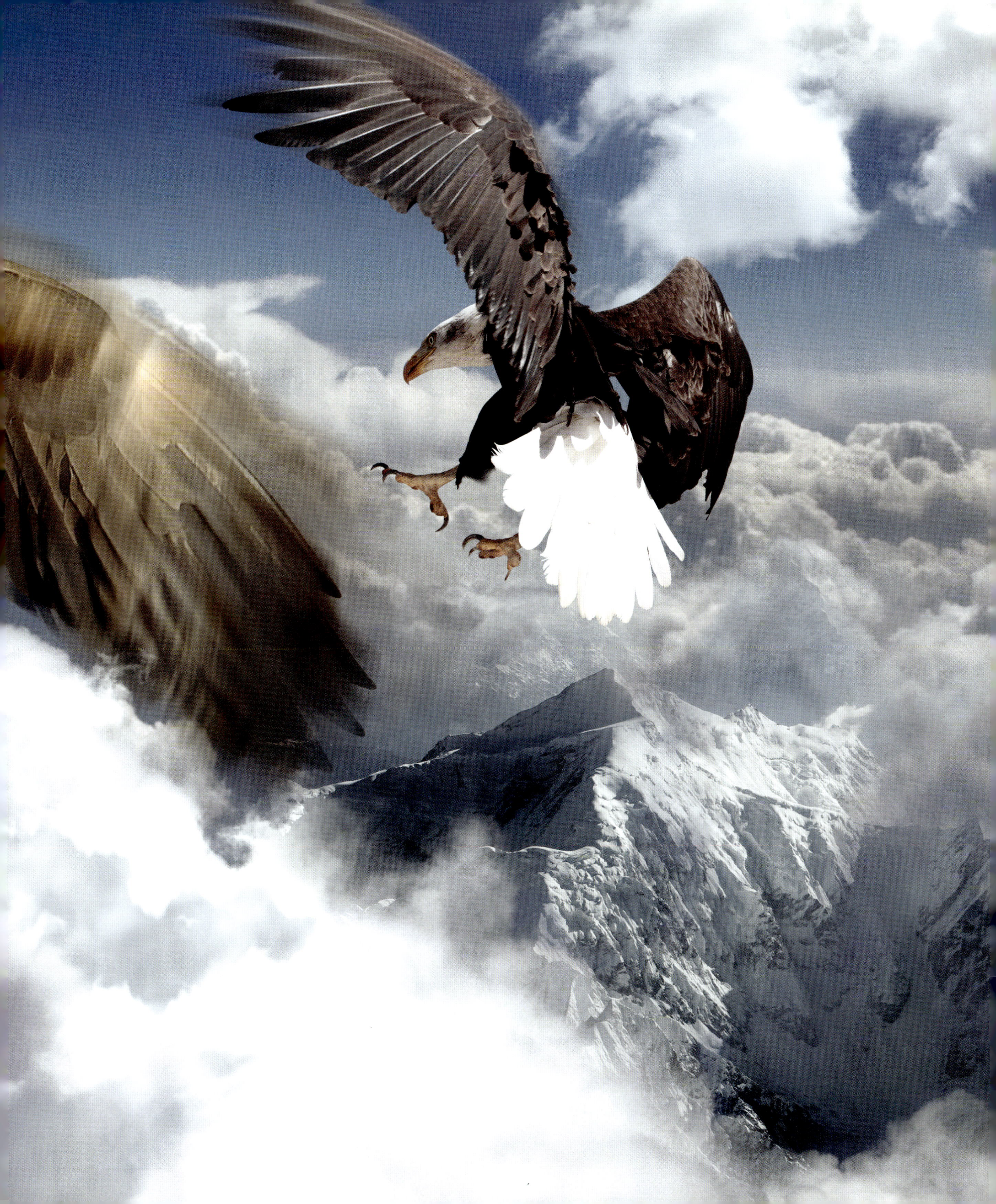

# SYLPHS OF THE AIR

Hidden in wisps of cloud or billowing mists, and carried on the wind, fairies are part of the very air around us. Some fairies are guardians of the elements, providing renewing rainfall or refreshing breezes. Other sprites can be more destructive, whipping up violent storms. Air fairies are seldom visible, seamlessly blending with blue skies, mist, rain and snow.

## WINDSTORM SPRITES

Tiny fairies called foletti love to stir up windstorms, riding on the backs of howling gales and shrieking with delight. If you listen carefully, their gleeful laughter can be heard above the noise of a downpour. These fairies sometimes gain entry to peoples' houses by creating a tiny whirlwind to transport them through a keyhole. Once inside, they can carry out all manner of mischief though they are rarely harmful.

# THE ICE FAIRY

The Yuki-onna, a Japanese sylph with a heart of ice, appears on snowy nights. Beautiful and serene-looking, this spirit of the air has flowing black hair and almost translucent skin. However, despite her loveliness, the Yuki-onna's eyes are said to strike terror in the heart of any mortal. Floating above the snow like a mist, this fairy leaves no trace. She may enter through an open window and lure victims outside where her breath turns them into icy statues. Other victims may simply be led astray as they struggle to find their way through a snowstorm.

*The sinister Yuki-onna fairy transforms her victims into icy statues.*

## FAIRY WINGS
# RARE SPECIMENS

*a collection of* WINGS *from the* FAIRY KINGDOM *found in meadows and woodlands across the world*

## WOODLAND SPRITE WINGS

Sprites found in woodland habitats show an astonishing variety of wing colours.

**ABOVE** *Of all sprites, the moss fairy's wings are amongst the loveliest.*

Throughout my years of travel across the world, I have gathered together a unique collection of exquisite fairy wings. From the brightly patterned wings of flower and meadow fairies, to the deep green or blue wings seen on woodland sprites, the rare specimens displayed here demonstrate the dazzling variety found amongst winged fairies. Although extremely delicate in appearance, fairy wings - like spider silk - are in fact incredibly resilient.

**ABOVE** *These wings are thought to belong to a rare mushroom fairy.*

**ABOVE** *These wings are almost certainly those of a stream-dwelling sprite.*

**ABOVE** *These will o' the wisp wings glow a deep red when night falls.*

**ABOVE** *The colour of a hawthorn fairy's wings changes with the seasons.*

## TREE FAIRY WINGS

Only a very few tree sprites possess wings. The specimens shown here are amongst the rarest in the fairy realm.

**ABOVE** *These maplefairy wings were found in New England, U.S.A.*

**ABOVE** *Featherleaf fairy wings, discovered in Mongolia.*

**ABOVE** *These cherry-blossom fairy wings glow on a full moon.*

## BEAUTIFUL BLOOMS

The fairies' magical powers are affected by the flora and fauna that surround them. Their most prized blooms are used for mysterious potions.

**ABOVE** *A bloom that has been touched by a fairy will always be full of powerful magic.*

## FLOWER FAIRY WINGS

Easily mistaken for butterfly wings, these beautiful specimens have a distinctive glowing appearance.

**ABOVE** *Found in Africa, these wings are those of the everlasting flower fairy.*

**ABOVE** *These cherry-blossom fairy wings glow on a full moon.*

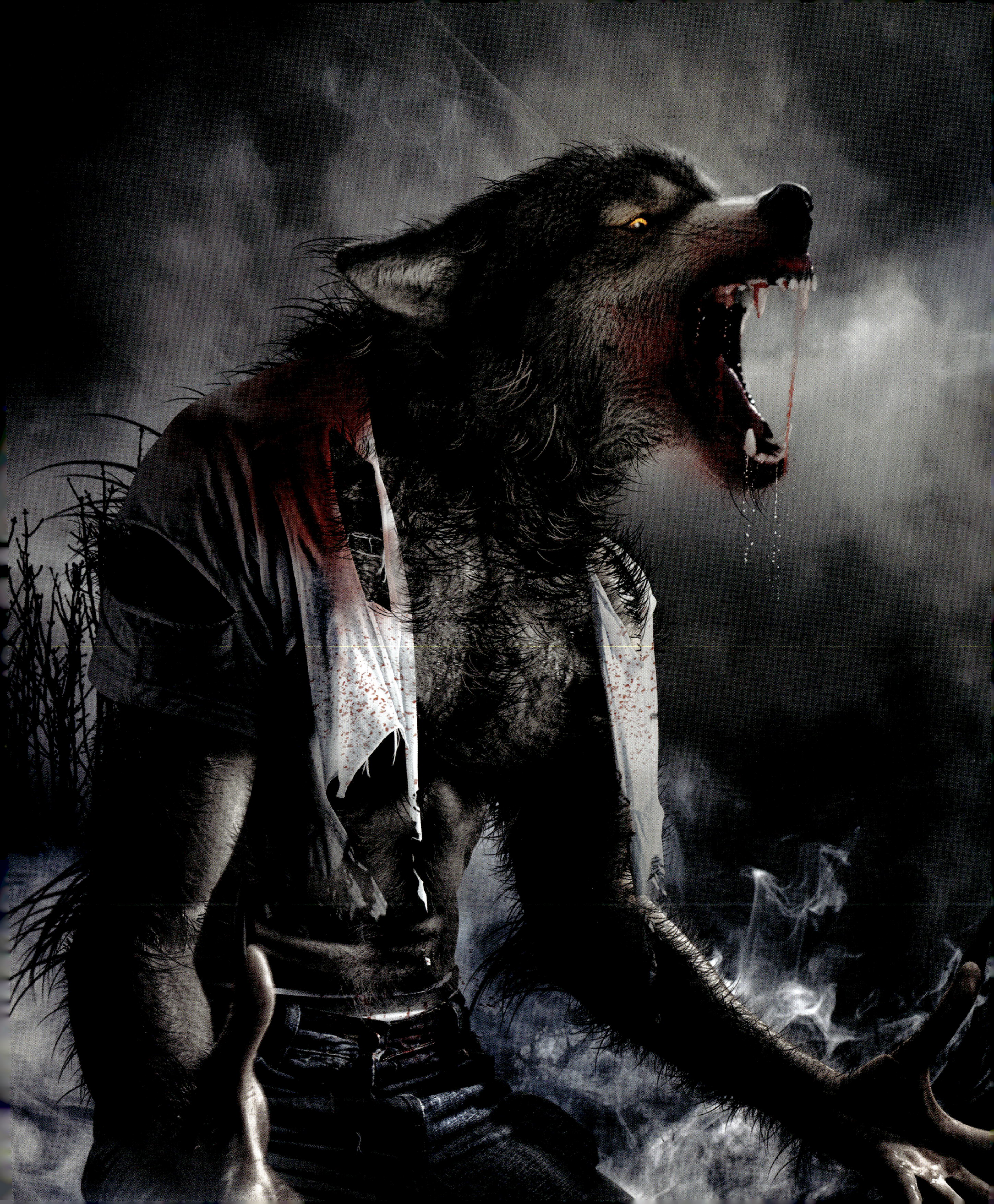

# CREATURES OF THE NIGHT

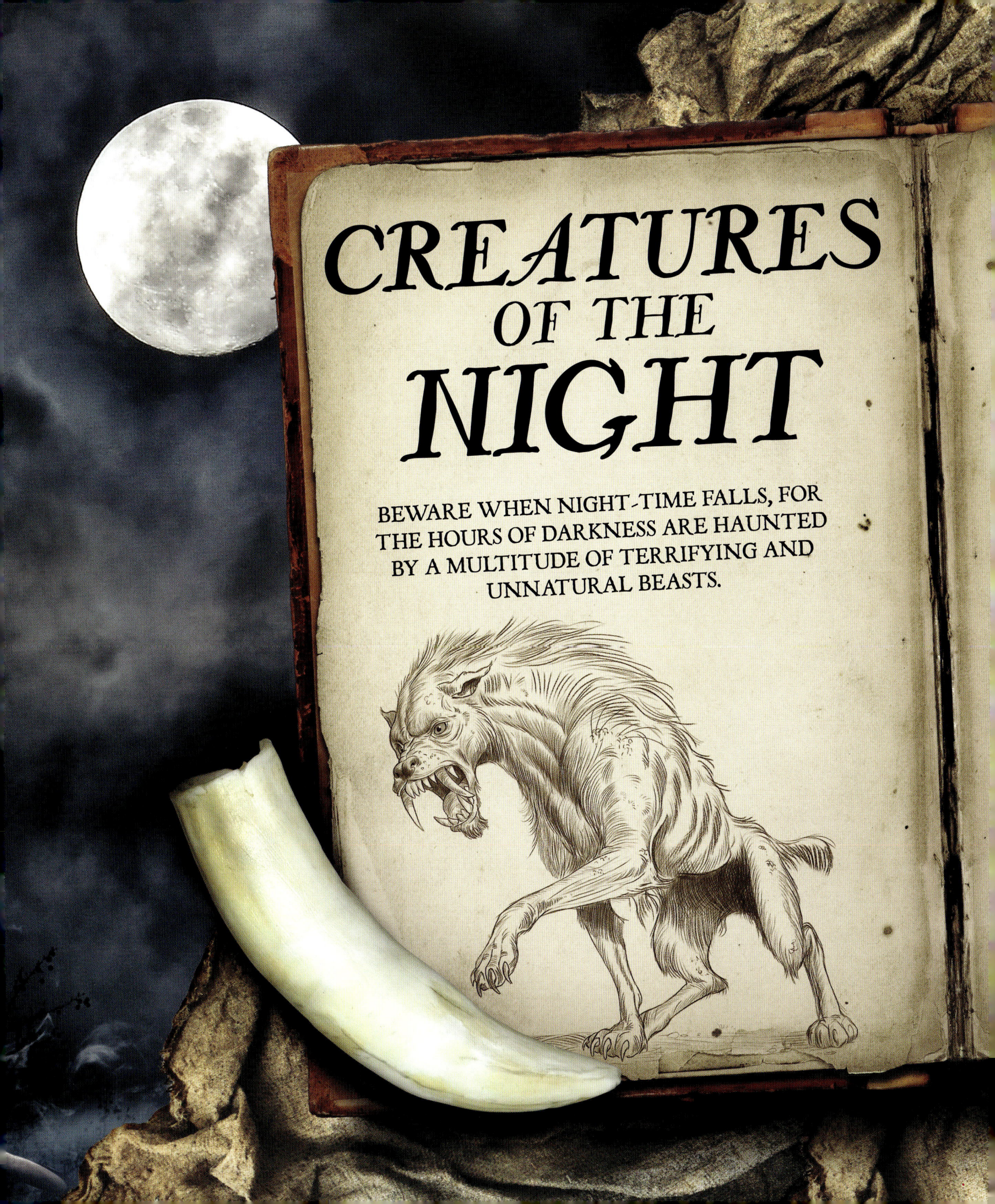

BEWARE WHEN NIGHT-TIME FALLS, FOR THE HOURS OF DARKNESS ARE HAUNTED BY A MULTITUDE OF TERRIFYING AND UNNATURAL BEASTS.

# THE WITCHING HOUR

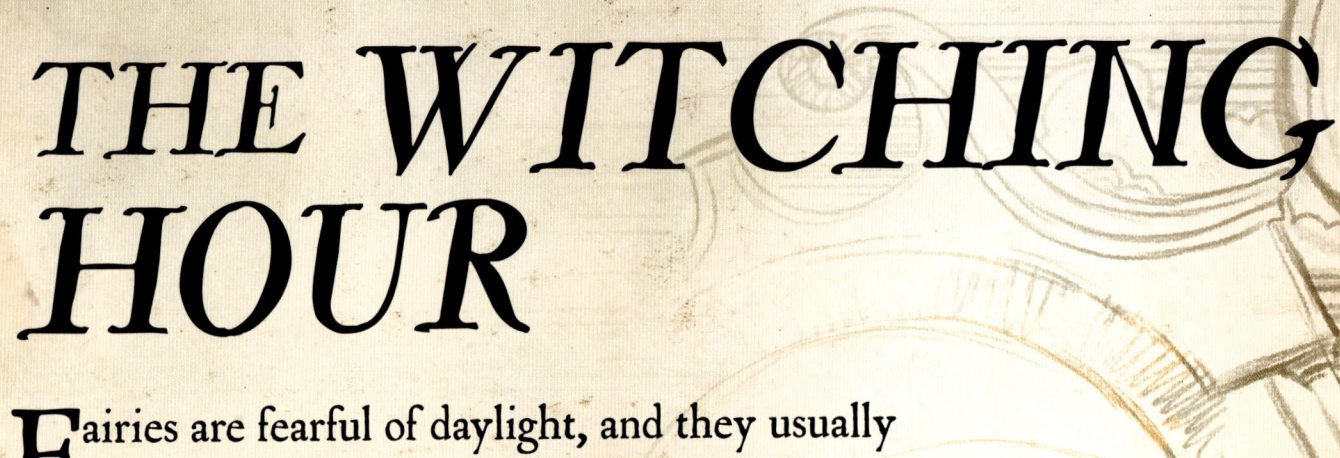

Fairies are fearful of daylight, and they usually emerge only between the hours of dusk and dawn. The most significant hour for fairies, though, is midnight. This enchanted hour, when witches fly and ghosts creep from the shadows, is when the magic of fairies is at its most powerful.

## FAIRY HORSEMEN

Perhaps one of the most frightening yet awe-inspiring sights for any fairy hunter is that of the "wild hunt". As midnight strikes on winter nights, a troop of fairies - accompanied by howling dogs - may be seen galloping across the night sky on ghostly steeds. Humans should remain safely indoors, for it is said that these fairies can suck the souls of the living up into the dark skies. Legend tells that the sight of the wild hunt is a bad omen, foretelling great misfortune - those looking to catch sight of the fairy horsemen must protect themselves by carrying something made of iron or a bunch of rowan berries.

*The rowan tree has many protective powers, and it is a good idea to carry a bunch of red berries or a knot of twigs to ward off the magic of bad fairies.*

When the winter winds blow and the Yule fires are lit, it is best to stay indoors, safely shut away from the dark paths and the wild heaths. Those who wander out by themselves on the Yule-nights may hear a sudden rustling through the tops of trees – a rustling that can't be the wind, for the rest of the wood is still...

— Kveldulf Gundarsson

*Beware the hour of midnight when fairy powers are at their most dangerous!*

## COCKROW

Careless fairies caught out after sunrise will be stranded in the human world until dusk. Many are turned to stone until night falls, when the spell is broken. Humans who chance upon a fairy statue should keep their distance, for touching such a stone can result in a painful "fairy burn".

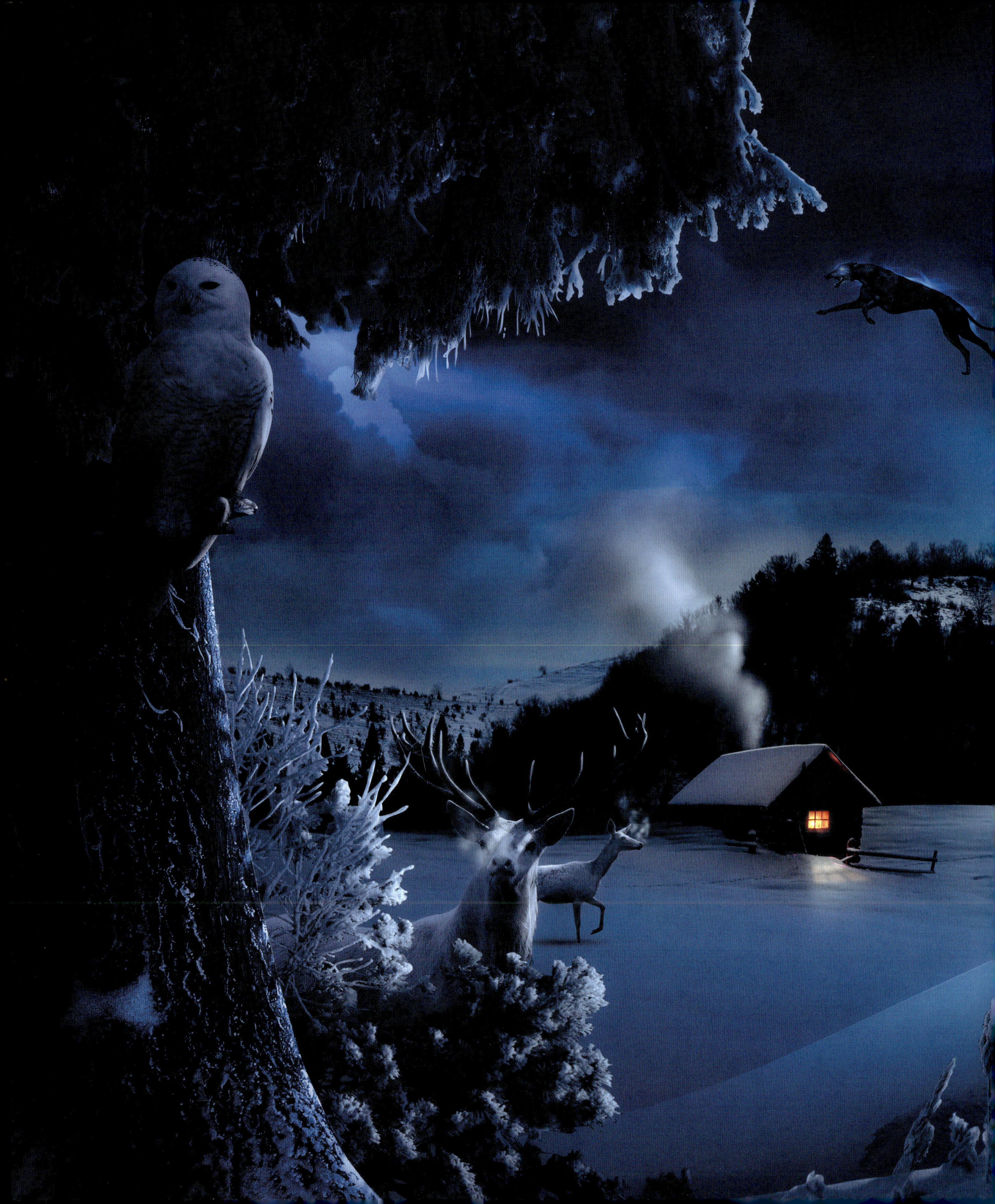

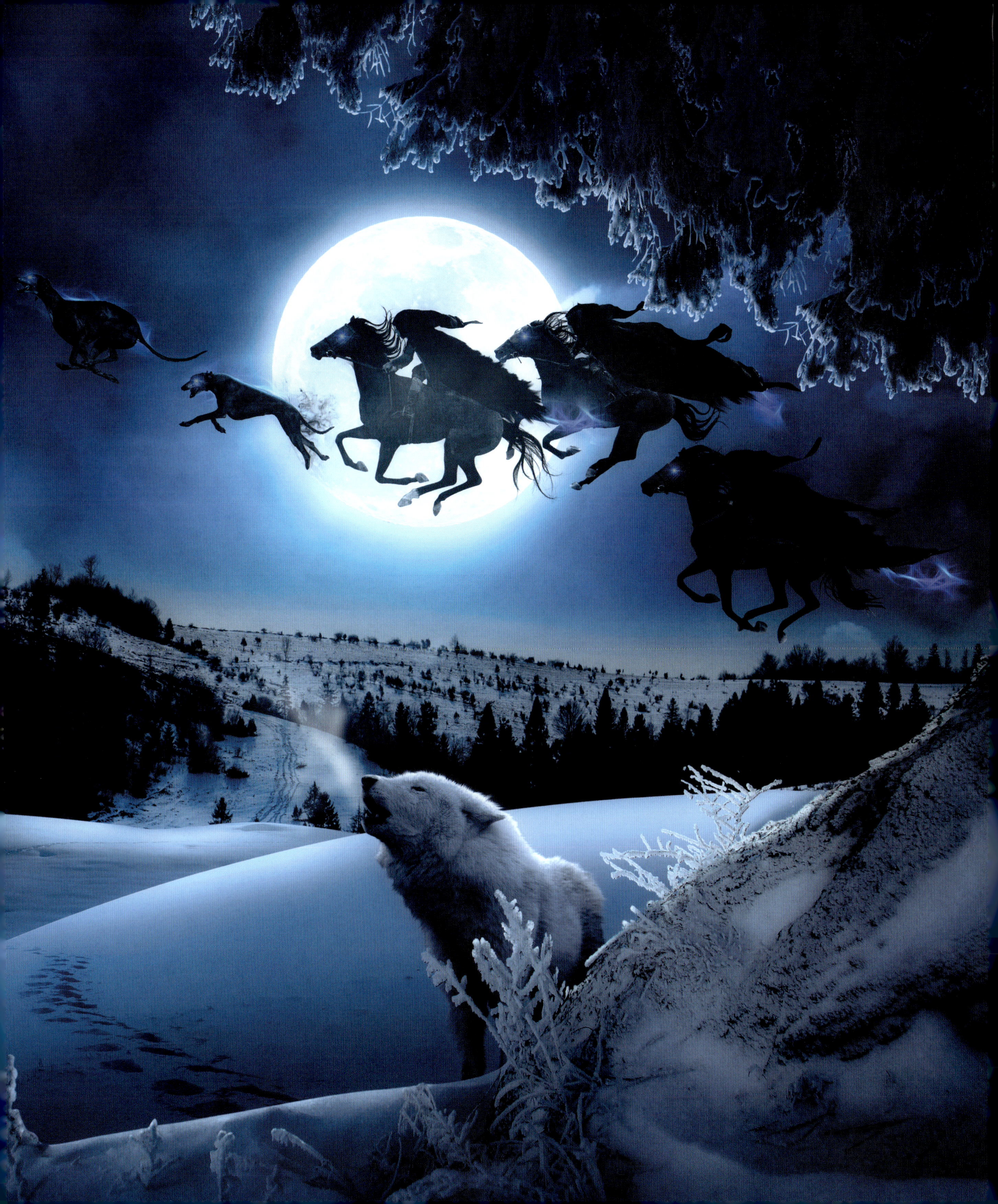

# THE WEREWOLF

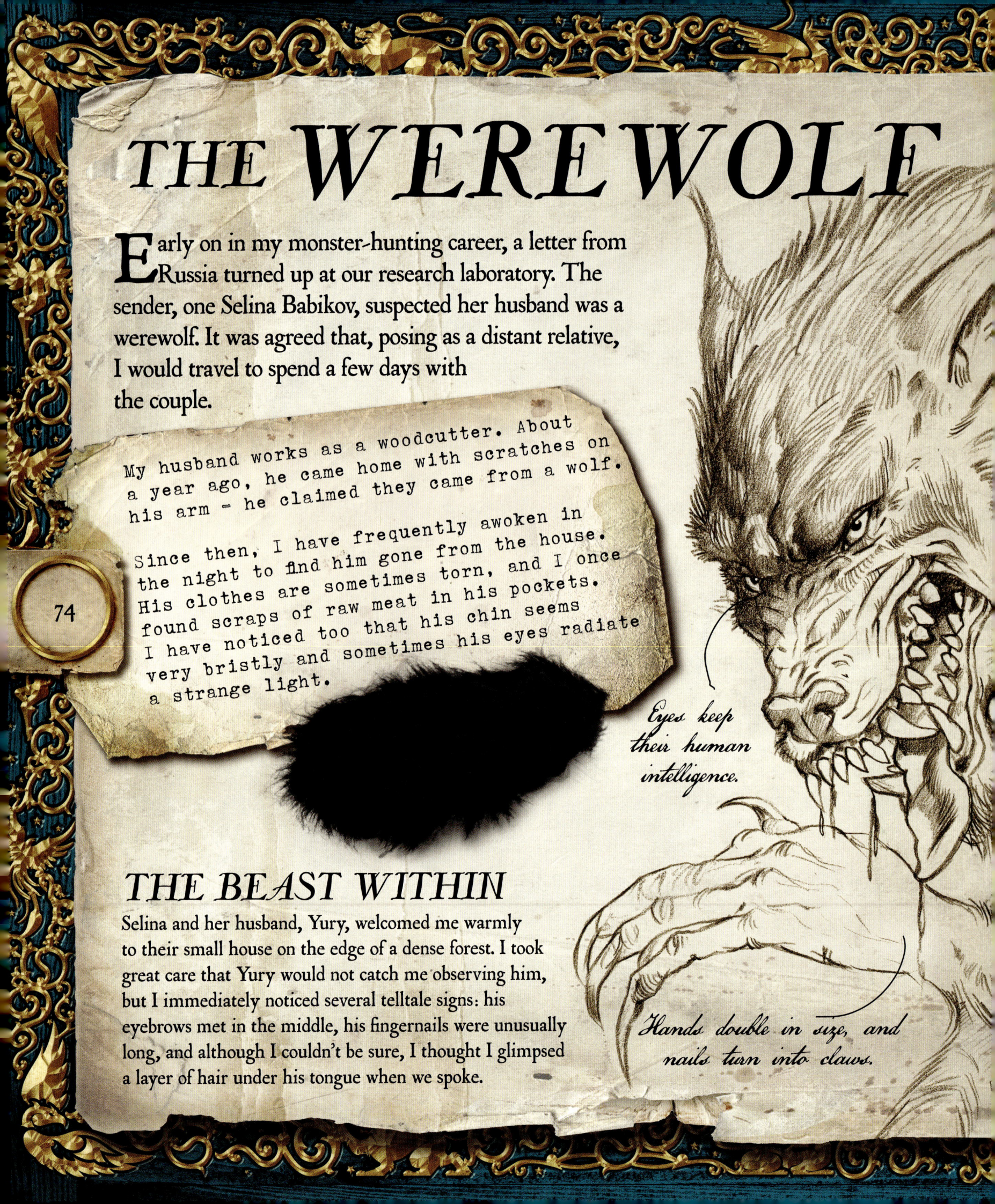

Early on in my monster-hunting career, a letter from Russia turned up at our research laboratory. The sender, one Selina Babikov, suspected her husband was a werewolf. It was agreed that, posing as a distant relative, I would travel to spend a few days with the couple.

> My husband works as a woodcutter. About a year ago, he came home with scratches on his arm – he claimed they came from a wolf.
>
> Since then, I have frequently awoken in the night to find him gone from the house. His clothes are sometimes torn, and I once found scraps of raw meat in his pockets. I have noticed too that his chin seems very bristly and sometimes his eyes radiate a strange light.

*Eyes keep their human intelligence.*

*Hands double in size, and nails turn into claws.*

## THE BEAST WITHIN

Selina and her husband, Yury, welcomed me warmly to their small house on the edge of a dense forest. I took great care that Yury would not catch me observing him, but I immediately noticed several telltale signs: his eyebrows met in the middle, his fingernails were unusually long, and although I couldn't be sure, I thought I glimpsed a layer of hair under his tongue when we spoke.

# Werewolf Study

Bones lengthen and muscle structure completely alters.

Ripped clothing is often a telltale sign.

Immensely powerful neck.

## Vital statistics

| | |
|---|---|
| Name: | Werewolf; lycanthrope |
| Description: | In human form: hairy; in wolf form: glowing eyes, ferocious fangs |
| Call: | A blood-curdling howl |
| Diet: | Raw meat, preferably human |
| Behaviour: | Frenzied; ravenous |

Could Yury be "cured" of this curse?

### 27 November

The moon is not quite full, but Yury seems restless. His eyes dart around and he seems unable to concentrate. At supper tonight, I was horrified to see him devouring a bloody steak in just a few mouthfuls.

### 29 November

Just after midnight, I heard a noise outside. Peering through the window, I saw Yury stepping quickly towards the dark forest. The man looked up at the full moon and then let out an unearthly howl. His hands began to claw at his clothes, fangs erupted from his jaws and fur grew all over his body. And then this terrible wolf-beast disappeared into the trees...

How exactly does the moon cause this change?

A bite from a wild wolf may pass on the werewolf curse.

## Werewolf transformation

The change from man to beast must be very painful!

75

# THE BOGEYMAN

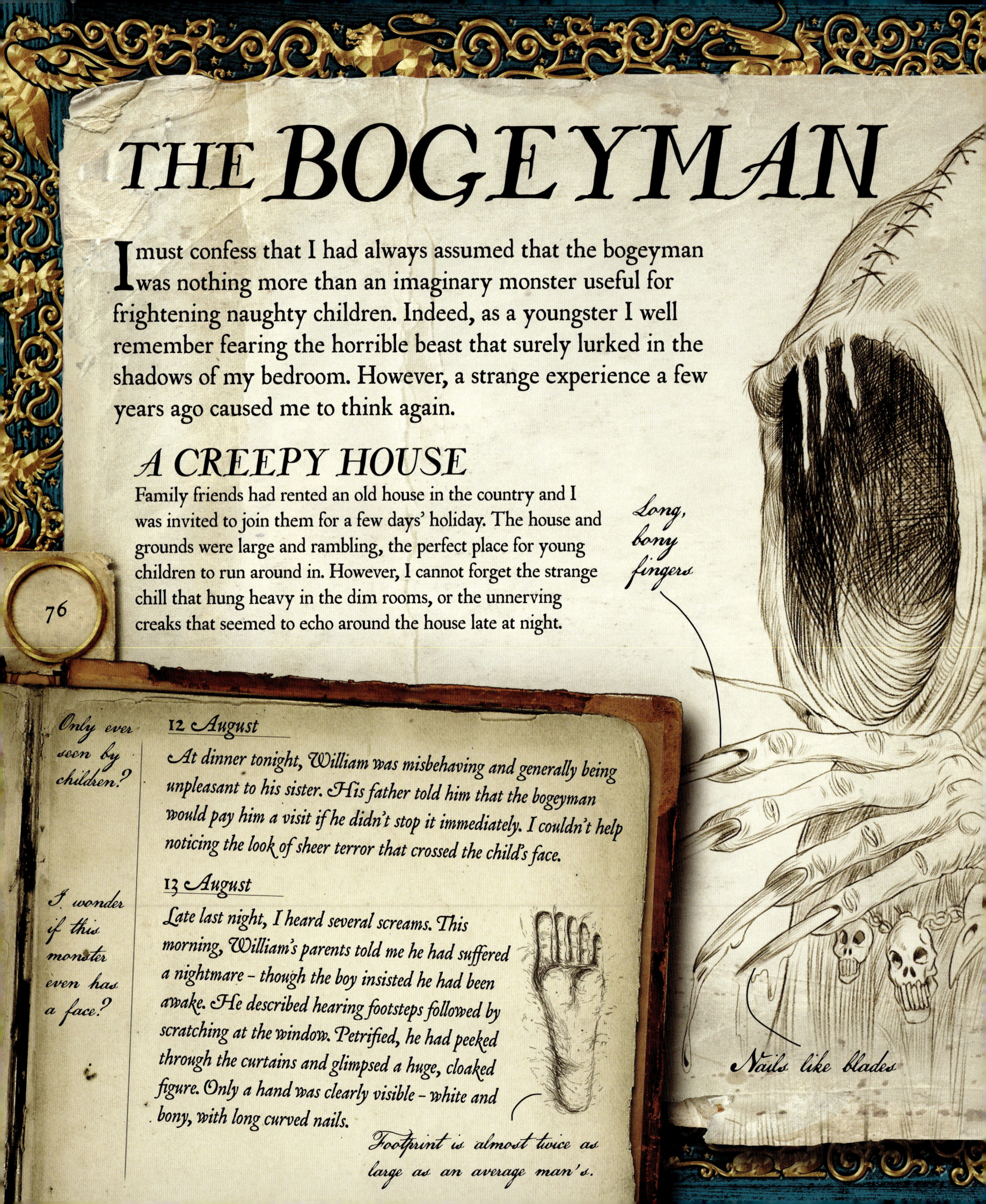

I must confess that I had always assumed that the bogeyman was nothing more than an imaginary monster useful for frightening naughty children. Indeed, as a youngster I well remember fearing the horrible beast that surely lurked in the shadows of my bedroom. However, a strange experience a few years ago caused me to think again.

## A CREEPY HOUSE

Family friends had rented an old house in the country and I was invited to join them for a few days' holiday. The house and grounds were large and rambling, the perfect place for young children to run around in. However, I cannot forget the strange chill that hung heavy in the dim rooms, or the unnerving creaks that seemed to echo around the house late at night.

*Long, bony fingers*

*Nails like blades*

*Only ever seen by children?*

**12 August**

At dinner tonight, William was misbehaving and generally being unpleasant to his sister. His father told him that the bogeyman would pay him a visit if he didn't stop it immediately. I couldn't help noticing the look of sheer terror that crossed the child's face.

*I wonder if this monster even has a face?*

**13 August**

Late last night, I heard several screams. This morning, William's parents told me he had suffered a nightmare – though the boy insisted he had been awake. He described hearing footsteps followed by scratching at the window. Petrified, he had peeked through the curtains and glimpsed a huge, cloaked figure. Only a hand was clearly visible – white and bony, with long curved nails.

*Footprint is almost twice as large as an average man's.*

*Hood covers face*

# STARTLING EVIDENCE

Not surprisingly, William refused to sleep in the same room again, and the rest of the holiday passed without further incident. However, the morning after the boy's "dream", I took a good look outside the bedroom and was startled to find very large footprints in the soil. There was also a series of deep scratches on the windowpane and I found a scrap of black material that had caught on the thorny bushes just below.

*Could this be the face of the bogeyman?*

## Bogeyman Study

*Abnormally long forearms*

### Vital statistics

Name: Bogeyman
Description: Cloaked figure; long nails (rarely seen, presence usually "felt")
Habitat: Under beds and in wardrobes; just outside the bedroom window
Behaviour: Nasty; delights in terrifying children

*Animal skull pendant.*

*Torn material from the bogeyman's cloak.*

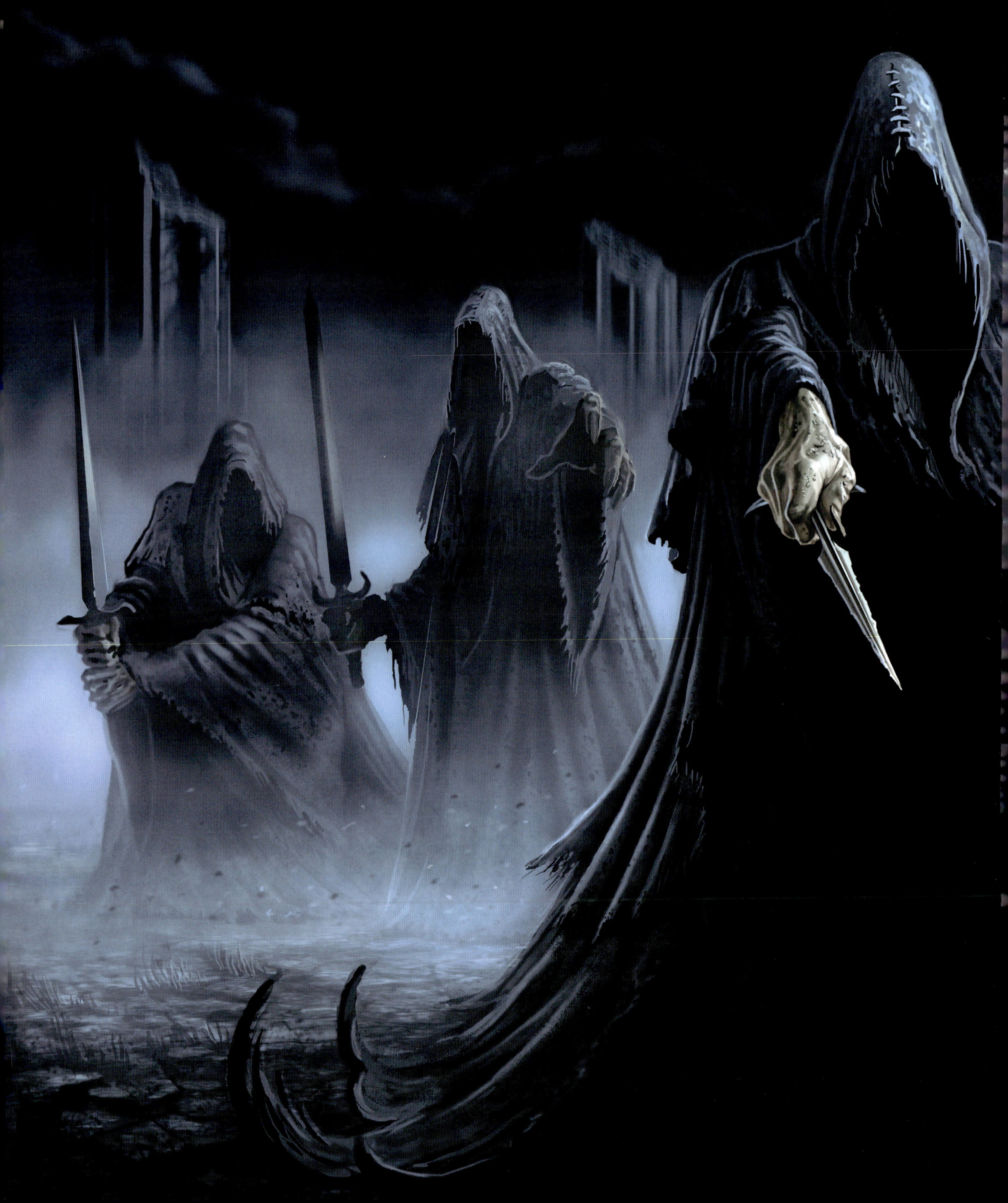

# SOUL-SUCKING GHOULS

Of all the creatures that haunt the hours of darkness, none can be more terrifying than these faceless horrors. As they roam across open countryside in search of human prey, their eerie cries might easily be mistaken for the moaning wind. Souls are sucked out of their owners and consumed in a matter of seconds.

# Acknowledgements

During my long career studying the beasts and fairies of the world, I have learnt much from the great beast hunters of ages past and present. They are too many to name here, but their knowledge and invaluable wisdom – often gained at considerable risk to their own safety – have been a constant source of inspiration to me.

In addition, I would like to extend my gratitude to all those who have made the writing and production of this book possible: my editor (and fellow beast enthusiast) Alexandra Koken; the designers Jake da'Costa and Russell Porter; WildPixel for Photoshop artwork; Leo Brown and Peter McKinstry for the illustrations; Ryan Forshaw for CGI artworks; and Yael Steinitz for production.

S. A. Caldwell

All images supplied courtesy of Dover Books, freeimages.com, iStockphoto.com, Shutterstock.com, Thinkstock.com with the exception of the following.

Alamy: 23 (top); /Heritage Image Partnership: 30–31; / PhotoAlto: 65 (bottom left)

© Carlton Books: 1, 2-3. 10-11, 12, 16-17, 19, 21, 24-25, 38-39, 48 (left), 51 (centre), 54-55, 62-63, 68-69, 72-73, 78-79

Getty Images: De Agostini: 22, 23 (top), 26 (bottom left); / Jason Edwards: 45;/Dave King: 42-43; /SSPL: 37 (bottom); / Steve Kaufman: 33 (right)

Every effort has been made to acknowledge correctly and contact the source and/or copyright holder of each picture and, Carlton Books Limited apologizes for any unintentional errors, or omissions that will be corrected in future editions of this book.

THIS IS A CARLTON BOOK

Text, design and illustration © Carlton Books Limited 2017

Published in 2017 by Carlton Books Limited
An imprint of the Carlton Publishing Group
20 Mortimer Street, London W1T 3JW.

All rights reserved. This book is sold subject to the condition that it may not be reproduced, stored in a retrieval system or transmitted in any form or by any means, electronic, mechanical, photocopying, recording or otherwise, without the publisher's prior consent.

The views contained herein are those of the author and do not necessarily reflect those of the publisher.

A catalogue record for this book is available from the British Library.

ISBN: 978-1-78312-296-7

Printed in Dongguan, China.